Moondust Memories

VAUGHAN STANGER

CONTENTS

INTRODUCTION

This collection of my short stories brings together eleven of my personal favourites. In no sense is it intended as a summation of my career to date or some kind of best-of. This is in part because not all of my published stories were available for inclusion, but mostly because such a judgement is not mine to make. A writer is probably the last person who should draw conclusions about the merits or otherwise of their work. So these are some of my favourites, nothing more, nothing less.

Ten of the stories collected here have previously appeared in Kindle editions. The odd-one-out is the final story in the collection, *Survival Strategies*. Originally published in the Canadian magazine Neo-opsis, *Survival Strategies* is significant because it supplied the seed for my novel-in-progress of the same title. The characters and events depicted in the published story appear, in a substantially revised form, in the early chapters of the novel. I trust the day will come when I complete it!

In the meantime, whether you are encountering these stories for the first time or the umpteenth, I hope you'll enjoy reading them.

MOON FLU

A screech from the long-suffering door hinges alerted me to the arrival of customers, an unwelcome distraction for a drowsy Cape afternoon. I placed my newspaper on the counter and glanced at the skinny, sharp-featured blonde and her dark-haired, athletic-looking partner. These tanned twenty-somethings gave off a faintly careworn air, as if they were taking a vacation but not enjoying it over-much.

In truth, quite a few years had passed since there was a whole lot to do around here. Once in a while a visitor might get to watch one of those new Deltas launch a satellite into low earth orbit. As for me, hearing that thunder rumbling up the coastline served as a bittersweet reminder of what might have been.

Not that the demise of manned spaceflight was uppermost in the thoughts of this couple, or so I reckoned. The man was studying the chalkboard menu with an intensity bordering on the feverish, while his partner was holding the door ajar, as if readying herself for a quick getaway. Her expression suggested she didn't fancy what was on offer. Doubtless the flyspecked windows and greasy table tops weren't helping. But the man looked like he needed a square meal and couldn't care less where he ate it. Feeling unwell might have been a factor too, judging by his sore-looking nostrils and the puffy skin around his eyes. My guess was confirmed by a succession of sniffles, each louder and more liquid than its predecessor.

"Jim, darling! Would you please stop doing that?"

I hadn't expected her posh English accent, though it did fit well with the look of disdain.

"Jeez, Phyllis, gimme a break! I've been driving for six hours despite feeling like I'm gonna die. Six fucking hours!" He held a tissue to his nose and blew loudly, which only made things worse, because a moment later his head tilted back and....

"Atishoo!"

"Bless you," said Phyllis.

"Moon flu!" I added.

The woman stared at me, her neatly plucked eyebrows beetling. Then she shook her head, presumably convinced that she had misheard. Jim looked too exhausted to care.

"Best find him some aspirin," I said.

The woman scowled at me. "Have you got any?" Her tone stung like acid. Jim, I reckoned, might not be overburdened with sympathy.

I gestured towards the door, waggling my thumb to the right. "The nearest mall is three blocks that-a-way. You'll find a drugstore there."

She gave me a withering look, which I met with a shrug. A glance at her designer jeans made me think that the local boutiques would not detain her long, but it was worth a shot for Jim's sake.

"Look, while you're gone, why don't I rustle up a double cheeseburger-and-fries for Jim here?"

Phyllis turned to him. "Will you be okay?"

"Yeah, I'll be fine."

"Right, I'm off then...."

The screech from the door hinges was followed seconds later by the screech of tyre-rubber on tarmac.

Jim sighed relief.

I smiled at him. "She'll have flashed her platinum Amex in more exclusive stores, but it might just buy you a bit of peace and quiet."

Jim grinned back at me. "Time enough to eat that cheeseburger you mentioned, anyhow."

"Coming right up." I scribbled his order on my pad, tore off the sheet and passed it through the hatch to Jerome. "Coffee?"

"Yeah, that'd be good."

I poured him a mug-full. "So, how long have you been suffering with this bug?"

"Oh, several days now." He sipped at his coffee before continuing. "Must have picked up the little fucker in New York. Sure wish I'd left it there!"

We both laughed: Jim at his own joke, me because I couldn't have cued up my favourite story any better if I'd tried. I leaned across the counter and waved him closer.

"That's nothing," I told him. "I once sent a bug on a much longer journey than that."

The way Jim shrugged as he took another sip suggested he was more interested in drinking his coffee than hearing my tale. But the steam must have tickled his nose, because his head tilted backwards again....

"Atishoo!"

"Moon flu!"

That was Al, my only other customer and a bit of a folk hero round these parts. Bald as a coot and freckled like a man who'd seen the sun close up and personal, he wore his seventy-plus years lightly. He winked at me and resumed eating his fried chicken.

Jim stared at Al, but since no explanation was forthcoming, he turned back to me.

"So what's with this 'Moon flu' business then?"

I waggled a thumb towards Al. The wall behind him was home to a collection of yellowing newspaper clippings plus a dozen photographs from the Apollo 12 mission.

"Oh, come on," said Jim. "Everyone knows that whole Apollo thing was a fake."

That was an opinion I'd heard a lot recently, though it never failed to infuriate me. I had moved to Florida from LA in 1983, just so I could live close-by the place I thought of as my spiritual home. Justifying the Apollo Project to West Coast hippy-folk had been difficult enough, but persuading their successors that the moon-shots hadn't been filmed in a Hollywood studio was proving a damned sight harder.

"Oh, really?" I could feel my face reddening. "Well let me tell you—"

But Jim wasn't about to let me get a word in edgeways.

"Jeez! I could have shot better footage with my Grandpa's cine camera!" He shook his head and sniggered, but was punished—or so I liked to think—with a volley of sneezes.

The first one got the usual response, but I didn't bother with the rest. By now, Jim was itching for an explanation.

"So, are you gonna tell me what this 'Moon flu' has to do with a couple of wannabe astronauts?"

Ignoring his jibe, I started my story.

"Remember what I said about sending a bug on a much longer journey?" I waited for him to nod before continuing. "Well, it just so happens that I sent that bug all the way to the Moon."

First Jim's eyes went wide; then his lips twitched while he worked on the math.

"You worked in the Space Programme during the Sixties?"

"Best years of my life."

Whereas working for General Electric in the Seventies had been anything but. Granted, the Nixon Plan had done wonders for the economy, but exporting televisions to South-East Asia hadn't compared with racing the Soviets to the Moon. I suppose the money had to come from somewhere, but it sure seemed a high price to pay.

Jim gave me an appraising look. "Ten dollars says you never was an astronaut!"

I patted both hands against my belly. "You can keep the money. I was no skinnier then than I am now."

"So what did you do?"

"Well, for one thing I helped build the camera that flew on Surveyor 3."

"Means zip to me."

"There's a picture of it on the wall."

Al turned in his chair and tapped a finger against the appropriate photograph. Jim wandered across the room to inspect it.

"Who's the astronaut?"

"That's Pete Conrad, third man on the Moon." Al's voice trembled with emotion. "That would be a damned hard shot to fake, I can tell you."

Jim rubbed his stubbly chin while he read one of the newspaper clippings, then he glanced at me.

"Brought back your precious camera, did he?"

"No, but the man who took the photograph did."

Jim gave a non-committal grunt. "Even if I believed you, I still don't see what it's got to do with this flu bug you keep banging on about."

Al scraped his chair backwards a few inches and got to his feet. He made a play of scanning the clippings, just for effect.

"There you go," he said. "Read this." He peeled the piece of paper from the wall and handed it to Jim. By the time Jim had finished the article he was staring at me in amazement.

"You sneezed into the camera?"

"It wasn't quite that simple."

"Oh, come on! Either you sneezed into it or you didn't!"

"May as well tell him the truth," said Al.

The sigh I let out was also part of the act.

"Well, I was just a regular lab technician, working for Hughes Aircraft Corporation. If someone told me to do something, I did it and no questions asked."

Jim nodded sympathetically.

"Anyhow, just hours before the camera was scheduled to be shipped out, my boss ordered me to open it up and clean out some contaminant detected by a test protocol I'd never heard of. Yeah, likely story! Much more likely I was doing the contaminating, I reckoned, since I was going down with a head cold at the time. Lying in bed that night, it wasn't too difficult to figure out who'd want to send bugs to the Moon. This was the height of the Cold War—and the military eggheads were always looking for an edge."

"You're jerking my chain, right?"

"As God is my witness!" I shook my head to emphasise the point. "And those eggheads got exactly what they were looking for. Two-and-a-half years of being bathed in cosmic rays must have done something to that bug's DNA, because two weeks after we got the camera back the whole team went down with something a damned sight worse than the common cold."

Jim nodded. "Moon flu, right?"

"Yeah, though it was no joke at the time. This thing was so dangerous it nearly killed me. I spent a month in hospital, but at least I got better. Three of my colleagues weren't so lucky."

"I bet the generals were impressed."

"Yeah, I reckon so." I lowered my voice a bit, as usual at this point in the tale. "Did you ever ask yourself how the Mekong Flu pandemic got started, back in '71?"

Jim shook his head. "Before my time."

"Well, Mekong Flu was supposedly even deadlier than Spanish Flu, which killed twenty million people after the First World War. Yet fewer than fifty thousand Americans died of Mekong Flu. Which is pretty amazing considering three million peasants died of it in North Vietnam, and as many again in South Vietnam, Laos and Cambodia. Was it just good fortune that we'd got our flu vaccination programme up and running in time? I don't think so!"

Jim's mouth gaped wide, though whether in amazement or disbelief I couldn't tell. A moment later I got my answer.

"Jeez guys, you almost had me going there! A flu bug that went to the Moon but came back a hundred times stronger? Yeah, right!"

A buzzer rang. Jim's platter was sitting on the rim of the serving hatch. I could hear Jerome sniggering in the kitchen. God (and Jerome) knew what he had done to that cheeseburger. I could guess, though. He had been suffering from a cold recently.

"Enjoy your meal," I said to Jim.

He was still chuckling as he grabbed the burger with both hands.

Not another word passed our lips until the door hinges screeched again. In came Phyllis, clutching shopping bags.

"Fast worker," I murmured.

Jim grunted while chewing a mouthful of cheeseburger.

"Don't worry, she'll catch that bug soon enough," I said.

He wiped crumbs from his lips. "Reckon it could be Moon flu?"

"You never know."

That made him chuckle; Al joined in too.

"What has he been saying about me?" Phyllis asked, glowering at her partner.

Jim winked at me as he slid an arm round her waist. "Some things that bug me never fly away."

She tried to wriggle out of his grasp. "If you've quite finished!"

He took one last bite out of his burger before planting a kiss on her lips. Phyllis responded with "Oh, yuck!" then wiped her mouth with the back of her hand.

Jim turned to me, sighed and placed a ten-dollar bill on the counter. "Keep the change. I reckon you've earned it." He feigned a sneeze then winked at me. "Moon flu!"

He was still laughing when Phyllis presented him with her bags. She turned on her heels and hurried out the diner. Something was still bothering Jim, though.

"Did it really happen? Apollo 12, I mean."

Al tapped a finger against the photograph of Pete Conrad and Surveyor 3.

Jim sneezed again.

"Moon flu!" Al got in just ahead of me.

Jim glanced at the photographs then shook his head. "Nah," was his final word on the matter.

The door hinges screeched one last time, closing out my story.

"You're batting none for seven this month," said Al.

"Yeah, I know. Idiots, the lot of them."

Al gazed at the photographs for a second or two then sighed like a man who had seen it all. Which he had, of course.

"I guess us old-timers will just have to cut the younger generation a little slack," he said with a sorrowful shake of his freckled head.

Which was pretty gracious thing for him to say, all things considered. And maybe it was time I faced up to reality, too. After all, with NASA disbanded decades ago and "astronaut" a job that no longer existed, Apollo doubtless seemed like the stuff of fiction to Jim. That four men had walked on the Moon would be difficult enough for him to accept, let alone that two of them had accidentally put an end to the Vietnam War.

Still, the irony was not lost on me, the man who sent that bug to the Moon.

Nor on Al, the man who brought it back.

SLICES OF LIFE

I woke up this morning with a head full of doggerel. The poem bore the stamp of youthful enthusiasm, if not of quality. A quick search through my diaries revealed that I wrote it on my sixteenth birthday. You would doubtless recognise the source of my inspiration, Leroy, if I recited that piece to you now.

There once was an artist who pickled a cow,
Then sliced it in half with a chainsaw.
He encased it in glass,
Did the same to its calf,
Yet was mocked for creating an eyesore!

In truth, I was never much of a poet, as you reminded me whenever you read my scribblings. Even so, those clumsy lines evoke the delight I felt on hearing that Mother and Child Divided had won the 1995 Turner Prize. The furore whipped up by the tabloids was sheer inspiration to a wild-child who delighted in raising hell in her GCSE arts class. Back then, Damien Hirst was to die for. Sound-tracked by Damon Albarn, of course.

Two years before Britart's finest hour, the State of Texas executed a murderer by lethal injection. Showing laudable, if ironic, concern for the future, Joseph Paul Jernigan donated his body to science. A magnetic resonance imager scanned Jernigan's cadaver, slicing him into pixel-planes thin as salami. The so-called Virtual Human was uploaded onto the Web. Some people thought the images macabre, others called them art. By papering the walls of your studio with them, you placed yourself squarely in the "art" faction.

Giddy with ambition and blitzed on acid, we brought our influences to bear on one outrageous project after another, melding digital media and roadkill into surreal installations that became a cause célèbre on the fringes of the British arts scene. But after four years of partying and three years of marriage, our relationship ended in acrimony. Once matters were in the hands of our lawyers, we never spoke again. With good reason I might add, for I had every reason to hate you, didn't I Leroy?

Until a week ago, I thought that the passage of time had blunted my anger, but I felt its familiar sting when I recognised your handwriting on that old-fashioned manila envelope. I was on the point of turning down your invitation when my Homebot relayed the news of your death.

As I walk down the long ramp that leads into the vast chamber of grey-painted brickwork and black-steel girders that houses the Tate Modern gallery, it occurs to me that I, Tanya Roberts, may be nothing more than an early work to be dusted off and put on display in the exhibition of your life. I feel sure that you are manipulating me, just as you did a quarter of a century ago.

Manipulated or not, I cannot help but be impressed by this, your ultimate creation. The hologram of a nude, middle-aged man towers over me, so tall that his scalp seems to graze the skylight. Your ruggedly handsome face is tilted downwards and your eyes are closed, as if the drone that suffuses the Turbine Hall has lulled you to sleep.

The cultural commentators have heralded this piece as your definitive bid for artistic immortality. To a world-famous artist afflicted with a terminal disease, the temptation to create some kind of grand summation of one's life's work must have seemed irresistible. But the title of the piece, You and Me in Disunity, is pregnant with implication. Perhaps that is why you invited me to attend a private viewing, before the cognoscenti descend en masse.

My mind conjures up a vision of the Turbine Hall swarming with the smug-looking, dressed-to-impress darlings of the Establishment, gossiping and name-dropping and guzzling champagne. I dismiss the image with a shake of my head, glad to have left that world behind.

Determined to obtain the best possible view of your hologram, I climb the stairs to the second level, then make my way to the barrier at the end of the platform. My head is at the same height as your feet, which float in mid-air ten metres from me. Only at this close range can I confirm my suspicion that your body has been sliced into sections, as if filleted by an invisible cleaver.

Hyperslice installations are nothing new to me, but the sight of a slice detaching itself from your thigh is enough to make me shudder. The slice spins on its axis as it spirals towards me, images flickering over its exterior like a magic lantern. I glimpse a gang of youths pushing a sports car along a rain-soaked street. A bottle of vodka passes from hand to hand, then pinwheels into the chocolate-orange sky. One of the voices is achingly familiar.

The slice lifts away before it reaches me, following a trajectory that will return it to your body. Presumably the incident it records dates from your late teens, a few years before we met. The thought that I might experience some of your subsequent memories makes me tremble.

In spite of my fears, I feel compelled to interact with the hologram, just like any member of my generation. I speak a few of the usual commands to no discernible effect. Sign language and arm waving also fails to stimulate a response. It seems that even in death you must retain complete control.

Amused rather than angry, I watch as a second slice peels away from your body, this time from the groin. As the slice settles over me, insubstantial as a soap bubble, I'm reminded of that moment of profound emptiness one experiences when an orchestra is about to strike up. Then, as if on cue, your sensory impressions engulf me.

The woman who has caught your eye at the Students Union disco is almost unrecognisable to me. Her voice is too strident, her eyes too wild. And as for her hair! If I remember rightly, that crimson dye-job was an attempt to emulate the singer of my then-favourite indie band.

Fuelled by cheap vodka, we dance for hours to the latest Britpop tunes and end up in bed. Next morning, the black-and-white photographs that adorn your bedroom walls catalyse the woozy afterglow of our one-night stand into a full-blown relationship. Pablo Picasso, Andy Warhol and Damien Hirst seem to be vying for artistic supremacy amidst a mosaic of press cuttings that celebrates the icons of Formaldehyde Art.

In truth, I was seduced by your influences.

Contrary to expectation, our relationship thrived. The sex was amazing, messier than a Jackson Pollock. A year passed before we began throwing crockery at each other. An argument about contraception provoked that first fight. I sport a tiny scar just below the bridge of my nose as a memento.

The barrage of teacups has just begun when, without warning, the slice pulls away. Twitchy with anticipation, I wait for the next slice to free itself from your body. At first the background hum provides the necessary balm, like aural cotton wool, but soon the sound of whispering usurps it. The effect seems calculated to irritate me.

Another slice begins its descent, leaving a gap in your belly. Hopefully, this one will not pick up the story where the previous one left off...

I needn't have worried. For me, this was the highpoint of our entire relationship. You must have felt the same way too, judging by the warmth that permeates your memories. Perhaps that is why, this time, she really looks like me, sounds like me.

Four years after our first dance, we are honeymooning on the Atlantic coast of Morocco. Having bartered away the afternoon in the souks of Essaouira, now we are racing each other along a crescent of sand beneath glittering stars. Your deliberate trip sends me tumbling into the surf. Our goose-bumped limbs entwine, sublime as seahorses. The tang of brine mixes with the smell of sex. Your fingernails rake my back, sharp as razor shells...

The memory ends too soon.

At the time, I wanted that moment to last forever. I think you did too. Was this the memory you fixated on when the neural flush consigned your mind to oblivion and your memories to posterity? There is no way to be sure, but I wouldn't be surprised.

I glance up at your body, still haunted by the question. The next slice is easing out of your ribcage even as its predecessor binds back into your belly.

Once again, your memory of me clashes with my remembered self-image. Aren't pregnant women supposed to glow? Not me, apparently. As I offer up my belly to the ritual of the mid-term ultrasound scan, you see a woman who looks dowdy, undesirable, burnt-out.

Offended by your attitude, I make a concerted effort to ignore your impressions of the scene and concentrate on my own memories instead.

I remember squirming as the instrument head smeared gel across my belly. You squeezed my hand as if to remind me that I would not be allowed to skip this particular check-up. Ultrasound does not harm the foetus, the consultant had asserted in a tone that seemed to chastise the defiance I had shown nine weeks earlier.

At first all I could make out on the TV monitor were pulsing waves of dark and light grey. Then the image sharpened, revealing our child-to-be. She looked like a wax model that had softened in the sun.

As I turned my head away, I realised the consultant was frowning.

"Is she healthy? Is she normal? Is she...?"

Three days later, after a demoralising series of tests, we were called back into the consultant's office. He mentioned a virus that caused foetal malformations; the details passed me by. Finally, he suggested I have an abortion. I felt no remorse at the time, only relief. The foetus was microcephalic. Not viable.

The same was true of our marriage, as it turned out, though it would be another six months before I learnt that the hard way. But you knew already, didn't you?

You should try again, said the consultant, his gaze bisecting the two of us.

Needless to say, we did not try again.

The slice lifts away, leaving me to my tears. As I gaze up at your body, I notice that its successor contains a piece of your heart. The slice envelops me before I have a chance to steel myself for the trauma to come.

Two days before the opening of your first solo exhibition, you reveal its centrepiece to me. Within seconds our fists are dancing like alpha particles in the heart of the sun. Now that sex cannot bind us together, fission rather than fusion is the only possible outcome.

The critics hail Mother and Child—Blighted as your breakthrough work. That the public unveiling comes so soon after our break-up only adds to its poignancy in their eyes. They applaud the unflinching way you weaved our personal life into a hyperslice constructed from that first ultrasound scan.

My virtual womb contains an archive of scribbled notes, intimate emails and playful camcorder clips: a subjective record of four-and-a-half months of anxiety and anticipation. Pointedly, you leave an empty space inside the head of the foetus.

But while you were basking in the adulation of your peers, I was dissecting your computer's hard disk with an electric carving knife. I realised it was a futile gesture even as I pasted the slivers onto the walls of what was once our studio, for you were always meticulous in backing up your work onto remote servers. Even so, I felt much better for making that gesture, childish though it was.

Following our break-up, you produced a series of hyperslices that attracted universal critical acclaim, whereas I retreated into obscurity. I frittered away a couple of years in a rented studio in Brixton, fashioning barbed wire and horsehair into expressions of my anger. Finally, I summoned up the courage to exhibit a few pieces in one of the more fashionable London galleries. The derision of the critics extinguished my desire to create art once and for all. Instead, I decided to build a new life, a life that did not contain you.

A glance upwards reveals that the slice has returned to your body. By rights, it should be the final one, since we never met again. So why, then, has your head ejected another slice? No answer comes to mind during its descent. And if the whisperers know, they seem disinclined to tell me.

This time there are no images or sounds, no sensory impressions of any kind, only darkness and silence and emptiness. I close my eyes, preferring to contemplate a void of my own making. In doing so, I'm reminded of that powerful feeling of anticipation an artist experiences when something is about to emerge from nothing.

The whispering starts up afresh, distracting me from my meditation. Annoyed by the interruption, I open my eyes. A moment later my mouth gapes open, too. Now there are two holograms floating in the Turbine Hall, facing away from each other. The woman is middle-aged and naked, just like her companion.

I am still pondering the meaning of this apparition when your rich baritone emerges from the susurrus, urging me to tell my side of our story.

Realisation comes swiftly. Not content with portraying the disintegration of our relationship, now you intend to highlight my failure to emulate your stellar career. The comparison you make is a stark one; it was then and it is now. This pair of hyperslices is supposed to demonstrate that, artistically, I was nothing without you.

Oh Leroy, this is too much! I thought that my hatred of you was a thing of the past, but by re-entering my life, however vicariously, you have rekindled that feeling.

I turn away from the holograms, shuddering.

"Leroy was right all along..."
"In terms of creativity, Tanya was a lightweight."
"Do you remember her solo exhibition?"
The erstwhile whisperers are laughing now.
"Leroy was always the strong one..."
"Such a unique talent..."
"Such a sad loss..."

This isn't the private showing you promised me, is it Leroy? Oh, I don't doubt there will be a formal unveiling tomorrow, with the interminable speeches and ersatz emotions that such events entail. But you couldn't resist one last manipulation, could you?

"You can prove them wrong, Tanya."

The sound of your voice still makes me tremble, and not just because of the bad times. I, too, have memories that I treasure.

"You can do it, if you really want to."
"But why should I bother?"

It's a stupid question to ask a dead man, but your proxy has been programmed to give me an answer.

"No one, not even me, has created a hyperslice 'live' in front of an audience. Think of it as performance art, if you like. It will be your unique achievement, Tanya. Something for posterity."

Hundreds of remote viewers flicker into virtual existence as I return to my vantage point at the edge of the platform. These ghostly figures flit around the Turbine Hall, occluding each other in a frantic search for the optimum viewpoint. They behave as if my decision was never in doubt.

Very well then, something for posterity...

Inspiration buzzes through me like adrenalin, just like the old times. Guided by your proxy, I begin downloading files from my personal archive into the installation. The digital records of my life will have to suffice, for I have no intention of emulating your terminal mind-flush. Not now, not ever. But even though I cannot match your absolute commitment to art, there are elements I can introduce to this event that your devotees may find challenging.

You thought that I would load this blank hyperslice with my perspective on our time together, didn't you Leroy? Giving me the right of reply must have seemed fair to you, a final balancing of the books. The death of love observed from two irreconcilable viewpoints; the ultimate artistic collaboration. It must have amused you to think of the critics deliberating over which version of the Morocco sex scene they preferred. I have no doubt that mine would have been dismissed as a naive work, not fit to be compared with the ultimate achievement of the great Leroy Haines.

If that was your plan, I must apologise for not sticking to the script. But I have a quite different story to tell, one that is so much richer than yours.

My story tells of a new start and a change of direction. It tells of a woman who gave up art to teach English; who got lucky and met a man who would, in time, come to adore her. Most important of all, it tells of the three daughters they brought into this world.

There's Jennifer, her blonde hair streaming past bony shoulders, her eight year-old face beaming with pleasure as the playground swing lifts her high into the air.

And that's Emma, slimmer and darker than Jennifer, her typically serious expression breaking into a shy little smile as she receives a rosette at her first gymkhana.

And there's Katie, her face smudged with chocolate, giggling as she toddles around the garden, pursued by her father.

Already, I can hear peals of laughter echoing around the hall. Not that the verdict of the critics worries me in the slightest, not any more. What do I care if they think of my hyperslice as sentimental dross?

I stand on the platform with my head held high, waiting for the laughter to die down. It seems to take an eternity, but eventually a hush settles over the Turbine Hall. Moments later, the silence is broken by the sound of footsteps.

I greet my family with hugs and kisses. Emma and Jennifer wriggle free of my clutches, much keener to play with a hyperslice than to bond with its creator. Within seconds they have worked out how to replay the video sequences. "So embarrassing!" I hear Jennifer cry.

My husband slips one arm round my waist and tickles my hip, making me giggle. His other hand is tickling Katie, who is riding on his shoulders. Not for much longer, I fear, for she is growing fast. Time always forces us to give up those things that we want to cherish forever.

Leroy, I'm not one of those people who think of their children as works of art. But I do know for certain that they represent the only kind of immortality that matters to me.

TOUCHING DISTANCE

When I was a child I was terrified of the dark. From the moment my mother turned out the light, I would stare wide-eyed at the bedroom curtains while I waited for the black to turn to grey. Several minutes would pass while my eyes adapted to the gloom. Only then could I dismiss the bedroom demons and safely fall asleep.

Thirty years later, those demons found a way into my dreams. And it was the darkness I awoke to that brought blessed relief.

My belly itched so fiercely I felt certain I had developed a rash. Memories of Chicken Pox and Measles prickled in my mind, but I kept those childhood reminiscences to myself. During my first day at the Somatic Sciences Institute, I had wanted to appear fully focused on my assignment. In any case, there had been little opportunity for small talk.

"How does that feel?" asked Dr. Kenna.

Whenever she spoke an image of a middle-aged woman with a plain face and heavy-rimmed glasses popped into my mind. But whether this representation was true to her appearance, I could not say.

"Itchy but bearable," I replied.

Dr. Kenna grunted, which I took to be a sign that things were about to get worse. My guess was correct. Within seconds the rash had spread over my entire body.

"And now?" she asked.

"The effect is stronger on my hands and chest, weaker on my arms and legs."

"That is not surprising, Mr. Markheim," she said. "Your skin is more sensitive in some places than others. Please be patient while I normalize the stimulation pattern."

After half-a-dozen adjustments, the itchiness felt much more uniform. "That's a lot better," I told her.

"You may not think so in a minute or two."

Her comment was typically cryptic. From the start, Dr. Kenna had given me the impression that she preferred to interact with her computer than talk to a human being. That she tolerated my presence seemed to boil down to two factors. Firstly, being blind, I was the ideal person to test her tactile body suit, which she claimed was a vital component of the personal sonar system being developed elsewhere in the institute. Secondly, with her funding almost used up, she was desperate for any kind of help. In fact, I had been happy to volunteer. When Dr. Chalmers mentioned the *Persona* project at my case review, it had seemed the perfect opportunity to shake off the torpor that had afflicted me ever since my accident.

Dr. Kenna cleared her throat. "Are you ready for the next stage?"

"Ready when you are."

This time, a wave of itchiness rippled over my body like an army of ants. I squirmed in disgust.

"Stand still, please. This will not take long."

I counted each second of my torment, reaching thirty before the ants stopped moving.

"All done." Said like a dentist comforting a child.

With the test completed, the urge to scratch myself was irresistible. But Dr. Kenna must have guessed my intention, because she grabbed hold of my hands, thereby averting any risk of damage to the gloves or body suit. I took a deep breath and tried to recover my composure.

"What is this stuff?" I asked, wiggling my fingers.

She let my hands slide out of hers. "Government scientists have designated it a 'smart material'." She spoke the words with pride, as if the link with the Establishment served to validate her work.

"Does it look good on me, then?"

My question drew a rare chuckle from her. "I'm afraid khaki is not really your colour, Mr. Markheim."

"Please call me Joe," I said for the umpteenth time.

"But the good news, Mr. Markheim, is that the tactile feedback supplied by the body suit should help you keep in touch with the world."

I was seven years old when I experienced blindness for the first time. Confined to bed after a bout of flu, I awoke one morning to find that my eyes would not open. My piercing screams roused my parents.

Mother bathed my eyelids with careful dabs of a spit-dampened handkerchief. After each gasping sob I was able to glimpse a little more daylight. With the last of the mucus wiped away, my world of primary colours was restored in all its glory.

But that night my dreams were full of darkness.

My second day at the institute began much as the first ended, with a lengthy session of calibration. Prompted by the computer, I traipsed along various predetermined paths around the laboratory, while Dr. Kenna tried to configure the imaging sensors to her satisfaction. For an hour or more, the laboratory echoed with her curses.

"That will do, Mr. Markheim," she said at last.

It was a relief to stand still, but Dr. Kenna seemed unwilling to permit me a break.

"Please turn to your right," she said. "Then take three steps forward."

As I completed the manoeuvre, I felt my right hip brush against something. I explored the space with my hands and discovered that I had bumped against the edge of a simulated workbench. The tactile illusion was surprisingly convincing; I could even feel the wood-grain as I rubbed my fingertips along the top surface.

"See what else you can find," said Dr. Kenna.

Chuckling at her lapse, I reached forward until my fingertips bumped against another object. The sensation was fleeting. I tried again. This time I achieved a firm grip on what felt like a plastic sphere, perhaps half a metre in diameter. As I rubbed my hands over its taut skin, I was reminded of a beach ball.

"Try throwing it to me," she said.

It seemed a ridiculous suggestion, but I lobbed the ball towards her anyway. Maybe the computer would intercept it on her behalf.

"Now try catching it," she said.

"You must be joking!"

"Just try."

I flapped my hands in the air, but to no avail. The ball tapped against my chest.

"That wasn't fair," I said.

"True," she said, sounding unconcerned.

I bent down and retrieved the ball. "Anyway, how will a virtual sense of touch help me perceive the physical environment?"

"That should become apparent when I activate the spatio-temporal projection system. In the meantime, please be patient."

Dr. Kenna resumed programming her computer, while I tried to imagine what she might have in store for me. Unfortunately, I failed to come up with anything pleasant.

"Ready when you are," she said.

I muttered my assent. A moment later, I experienced a prickling sensation near the top of my left thigh. Heedless of possible damage to the fabric, I rubbed at the spot. My fingertips found a pea-sized bulge.

For once Dr. Kenna ignored my faux pas. "Right, Mr. Markheim. The computer is throwing the ball ... now!"

The blip sneaked out from under my fingers and began ascending the left side of my torso. So rapidly did it move across my ribs and shoulder that I scarcely had time to swat at it with my right hand. This time the virtual beach ball collided with my left elbow. I stepped backwards, surprised less by the impact than its bizarre harbinger.

"Not bad at all," said Dr. Kenna. I understood that the praise was meant for her, not me.

After six failures, I succeeded in catching the beach ball, an achievement that pleased me despite its absurdity. Dr. Kenna's response was to bombard me from random directions, so as to exercise my new, omni-directional "vision" as thoroughly as possible. I dodged the projectiles as best I could, coerced by the blips that scuttled over my body.

Dr. Kenna's intention had finally become clear to me. Equipped with her tactile interface, my body would be transformed into a map of the world.

Throughout my teenage years I followed the path of least resistance, in the academic sense at least. Unlike my classmates, I relished the annual cycle of lessons and exams, which I felt certain would culminate in a degree in the Humanities from some metropolitan university. A career in teaching seemed inevitable.

The paths I followed through the local housing estate were selected with much greater care. I zigzagged across the roads, always seeking the shortest route from A to B. I counted the seconds, convinced that time was the only valid measure of distance.

A collision with a blind man jolted me out of my complacency. Even as I helped him to his feet, my mind was wrestling with the problem of what to do if disease or old age robbed me of my sight. Having given the matter considerable thought, I closed my eyes and taught myself to steer a reliable course through the darkness.

The thought that some irresponsible engineer might one day build a silent car filled me with dread.

It was mid-morning on the third day before the trials proper got underway.

"Please turn around and walk the length of the room," said Dr. Kenna.

"You will stop me before I hit the far wall, won't you?"

Having failed to provoke a response, I began walking. At first I sensed nothing unusual, just the cool touch of the floor against the soles of my smartly shod feet. Then, without warning, I felt a series of rectilinear shapes impinge upon both sides of my body. I turned back and forth, letting the edges scuff over my skin.

"Two rows of houses?"

"Close enough," she said. "You are walking along the main street of a small town. Please continue."

At first I could perceive only the basic structure of the scene: the outlines of buildings and the layout of the roads. But as I explored the simulation, I learned to focus on the fine detail of my body-map. By the time Dr. Kenna directed me into a shopping plaza, I had little difficulty in discerning the blips generated by lampposts and rubbish bins. I found myself wishing that their physical counterparts were as easy to avoid.

After what seemed like an hour, but may have been less, Dr. Kenna interrupted my wanderings.

"Please keep still while I reset the scenario."

The harsh outlines of the roads and buildings blanked out and then reformed. After a brief period of disorientation, I realised that I was standing at the edge of the plaza, roughly two metres from the kerb.

"What comes next?" I asked.

"Movement, of course."

Before I could respond, a tiny blip formed just above my right heel and started to climb up the calf muscle. It accelerated past the back of my knee, growing in size all the time, before traversing my buttock and hip. When it reached my belly, its trajectory reversed. Descent mirrored ascent, with the blip shrinking as it slid down the front of my leg. Five seconds later all that remained was a slight itch near the base of the shin.

A beachball could not have generated such a fast-moving signature—that much was certain. As I contemplated other possibilities, a sense of foreboding seeped into my mind.

"This time I am going to run the sequence with full sensory playback," said Dr. Kenna.

Traffic noise erupted from the speakers, accompanied by a whiff of exhaust fumes. I heard the swish of tyres on a wet road. The sound was exactly the same as on the day I was knocked down by a car.

I was fifteen years old: more thoughtful than most of my peers, yet still prone to odd moments of inattention.

The rain was dripping down the back of my neck as I performed my kerb drill. I spotted a gap in the traffic, but in my haste I forgot to look over my right shoulder. When I stepped into the road, a left-turning Austin 1100 knocked me off my feet like a rugby fullback tackling a winger. I landed on my backside, having flown just far enough to avoid a second impact.

Dazed but unharmed, I clambered to my feet and wiped the splashes of mud from my grey flannel trousers. The driver got out of his car, lingered just long enough to ascertain that I was uninjured, before driving off towards Chatham town centre.

A more considerate driver offered me a lift home. Sitting in the back of his Ford Cortina, I consoled myself with the thought that if I ever did lose my sight I would take much greater care when crossing a road.

By the fourth day, the repetitive nature of Dr. Kenna's experiments was becoming tiresome to me. I had been standing on the pavement of her anytown for what seemed like hours, monitoring the traffic as it flowed up and down the High Street. Although the presence of moving vehicles no longer made me shudder, I found the idea that we might continue in the same vein for another four weeks depressing to say the least.

"That will be all for today, Mr. Markheim," she said.

I felt the tension drain out of my muscles. Thank goodness, I muttered under my breath.

The traffic noise decreased in small steps as each vehicle was deleted from the simulation. Finally, only a single blip remained. Strangely variable in shape, this lone survivor of Dr. Kenna's purge continued to creep up the inside of my right calf. I decided not to report my observation, for I was sure she would eliminate the anomaly when ready.

"More of the same tomorrow?"

Dr. Kenna cleared her throat. "No, we must push ahead as fast as possible. Tomorrow, I want to introduce some pedestrians into the simulation."

The prospect made me feel sick in my stomach.

"There is no reason to worry, Mr. Markheim." She must have noticed my discomfort, for her tone was more soothing than usual. Even so, her words failed to reassure me.

The previous afternoon, I had described precisely this scenario to Dr. Chalmers. He told me that he understood my misgivings, but recommended that I continued to participate in the trials. After a lengthy argument, we agreed that I should return to the laboratory.

Now that my worst fears had been confirmed, I turned once again to mental rehearsal. I tried to imagine the tactile signature a pedestrian would generate as it walked along the street. The scissoring pattern I came up with seemed strangely familiar. My heart missed a beat when I realised that the blip crawling up my leg was morphing in exactly the same way.

"Dr. Kenna, why did you lie to me?"

"What are you talking about?" She sounded nonplussed.

"You know damned well what I'm talking about! Your simulation already contains a pedestrian." I gestured in the direction indicated by the blip. "It's walking along the pavement on the other side of this road, about thirty metres from here."

"Mr. Markheim, there are no pedestrians in this version of the simulation, only vehicles. And I have deleted every one of them already."

I double-checked my body-map. "There is a pedestrian. And it's getting closer all the time."

I heard the sound of equipment being clipped together. When Dr. Kenna spoke again, her voice sounded muffled, presumably because she was wearing some kind of VR headset. "I have just entered the simulation," she said. "Please monitor my movements while I walk around the plaza."

Her tactile signature began creeping across my abdomen, morphing continuously. When she had completed one circuit, I reported my findings.

"At the moment, you're located roughly ten metres to my right, moving in a clockwise direction."

"Good, that proves that the projection system is working correctly." She sounded relieved. "Is that other signature still present?"

"No; it has gone now." I felt relieved but annoyed too, for now Dr. Kenna would be even harder to convince.

"Are you sure it was there in the first place?"

"Definitely!"

"I could try boosting the tactile output ..."

I gave my consent before she could change her mind.

After the adjustment my skin was prickling more fiercely than ever, but the detail in my body map was noticeably sharper. Unfortunately, this enhancement had come too late. There was no sign of movement anywhere in the scene.

"Still nothing," I gasped.

I heard Dr. Kenna pacing around the laboratory. "It was probably just a system glitch," she said after a few seconds. "There's nothing to worry about."

Her explanation didn't convince me at all. I was sure I'd found a ghost in Dr. Kenna's machine.

That night I dreamt of a woman who stood at the foot of my bed, shrouded in darkness, silent as death. I cowered beneath her implacable gaze, begging for release. After what seemed like an eternity, she stumbled forward like a marionette released from its strings. Her lacerated face loomed over me, dripping blood onto my skin, where it fizzed momentarily, leaving behind a rash of blisters. One by one, they started to burst ...

Overcome by panic, I tumbled out of bed, dragging the bedclothes with me like a demented ghost. When my hip collided with the door handle, some obsolete instinct made me fumble for the light switch, an action that illuminated the state of my psyche, if nothing else. I held my breath, counted to sixty and regained my composure by slow degrees.

The itchiness wore off, but sleep would not come.

On the fifth day, Dr. Kenna populated the simulation with a crowd of pedestrians. I pleaded with her to give me more time to prepare, but she reminded me that the project's deadline was drawing near. An hour would pass before I ceased flinching in the presence of my virtual brethren.

Dr. Kenna cleared her throat. "I am going to reintroduce the traffic now."

I sighed with relief. Compared with the movements of pedestrians, the vehicles traversed my body with pleasing predictability.

After I reported my observations, Dr. Kenna directed me to face a group of pedestrians who were standing next to a bus stop. As I turned around, the quartet of blips migrated around my right hip. But when the formation stabilised I noticed that one of the blips was missing.

"Your projection system doesn't seem to work properly at certain angles," I told her, feeling rather smug.

I heard her speak to the computer. A moment later, the missing blip reappeared in a location guaranteed to get my full attention. I rubbed my groin gingerly.

"You have just experienced the optional projection mode for head-on trajectories," she said tartly.

And I had just experienced one of Dr. Kenna's rare flashes of humour.

The trials resumed. Before long, I found myself envying the pedestrians; unlike me they did not suffer from boredom.

A glancing contact snapped me out of my daydream. I took a step backwards, then another, but failed to disengage from the pedestrian. It seemed unable—or unwilling—to let go of my arm.

"Is the simulation operating normally?" I asked, aware that I was trembling.

"Yes, of course it is," replied Dr. Kenna.

"So why hasn't the pedestrian released me?"

There was a brief pause while Dr. Kenna interrogated the computer. "The nearest pedestrian is three metres from you," she said. "Are you quite sure you experienced a collision?"

As if on cue, the pedestrian let go of my arm. I spun around with my arms outstretched, but failed to make contact with my assailant. Concentrate on your body-map, I told myself. The reminder came too late though, for now there were several pedestrians nearby—and their tactile signatures all felt alike.

"What happened there?" Dr. Kenna asked.

"I think yesterday's 'system glitch' has returned."

She clicked her tongue loudly. "I cannot afford another wild goose chase, Mr. Markheim."

"Nor can you afford to conduct these trials using an unreliable simulation."

This time there was no response from Dr. Kenna. Satisfied that I had her full attention, I continued: "I want to find out why the pedestrian attacked me. Will you help?"

"I seem to have little choice in the matter," she said, sounding weary. "So, what do you want me do?"

"You can start by boosting the body suit's tactile output to its maximum setting."

"That would be risky."

"Just do as I ask, please."

"If you insist."

Pain erupted everywhere at once, as if my entire body was being consumed by fire. But within seconds the sensation had diminished appreciably, indicating that my nervous system had adapted to this extreme level of stimulation.

"Now delete every moving object," I said.

Dr. Kenna complied without comment. As each signature was erased from my body-map, I experienced a localised reduction in pain. By the time I had counted to thirty all but one of the blips had disappeared. I made no attempt to retreat from the pedestrian as it walked towards me. Instead, I turned to face the road. A moment later I felt a pair of hands resting against the small of my back. My hunch was correct: the pedestrian wanted me to step into the road, in front of an oncoming car. But this would be no mere replay of an accident from my childhood, I realised. Instead, a much more recent incident was about to be re-enacted.

"Have you located the pedestrian?" asked Dr. Kenna.

"To be precise, she has located me."

"Mr. Markheim, the pedestrians have no gender attributes. So why do you perceive this one to be female?"

"Read my case notes, if you haven't done so already. You will find the answer there."

She said nothing, which to my mind was a tacit admission of her collusion with Dr. Chalmers. But tempting though it was to berate Dr. Kenna for her duplicity, I knew that my own guilt was paramount now.

"Dr. Kenna, please program the simulation so that it contains a single car travelling at fifty kilometres per hour along the north-bound carriageway."

"Anything else?"

"No, that's all. When the simulation is running, please cue me in fifteen seconds before the car is due to pass my current position." I felt the hands touch my back again, as if to remind me that I had my own part to play. "And don't interfere, whatever happens."

Dr. Kenna grumbled to herself, but the lack of overt resistance suggested she was willing to obey my instructions. A brief session of verbal programming ensued, after which she declared the simulation was ready.

Hugging myself tightly, I tried to summon up what little courage I possessed. I told myself that what was to come had happened before, that I had lived through it once and would do so again. The thought provided little comfort though, for this time I would be experiencing the incident from a quite different standpoint. The prospect terrified me, but I realised that I had entered into a tacit agreement that could not be revoked at this late stage.

"Start the run," I said.

"The car is moving towards you." Dr. Kenna sounded relieved that she had relinquished control of the scenario. "Fifteen seconds to closest approach. A pause then: 10 ... 9 ... 8 ..."

Her voice lapsed into silence. Not that it mattered, for I had long ago learned to conduct a flawless countdown in my head.

Five ...

Engine noise growled from the speakers, building to a crescendo of fear.

Four ...

The tactile signature ascended my tingling body, mapping out the fatal trajectory.

Three ...

I turned to face my nemesis, masking it with my blind spot.

Two ...

Trembling with terror, I fought the urge to jump clear.

One ...

Trapped in a freeze-frame of anticipation, I begged for forgiveness.

Zero!

The impact was a stinging, body-wide kiss.

I lay on the road, curled up in a foetal position, listening to the car accelerating into the distance. Dr. Kenna knelt beside me and rested a hand on my shoulder. I shrugged off her assistance and got to my feet. I stood in silence with my head bowed, while I tried to come to terms with the fact that I was unhurt.

In real life, the pedestrian had not been so fortunate.

I should not have been driving that morning, not in my flu-ridden state. I remember mopping my face with a sodden handkerchief and thinking that if my car's ventilation system could demist the windscreen, then surely the cold-cure I had taken an hour earlier should have done the same for my streaming eyes.

The accident happened while I was driving along Maidstone road, a few hundred metres north of Chatham railway station. I was approaching a pedestrian crossing when a fierce itch inside my nose triggered an uncontrollable bout of sneezing. As my eyes blinked shut, my hands jerked free of the steering wheel. I stamped on the brake pedal, but the car skidded on the slippery tarmac. I heard a shouted warning, but too late, too late ...

The woman never regained consciousness. Three months after her death and a week after my conviction for dangerous driving, I became blind overnight. Following a series of tests, mostly of a psychological nature, I was referred to Dr. Chalmers, who diagnosed my condition as "psychosomatic blindness."

In truth, I had chosen not to see.

I have been lying on this bed for hours, trying to resist the onset of sleep. My mind is buzzing with anticipation, my skin prickling no less fiercely.

Dr. Chalmers has diagnosed my condition as tactile tinnitus, an epidermal reaction brought on by prolonged exposure to high levels of stimulation. For that I can blame Dr. Kenna—and also, perhaps, my own impetuosity.

One week after the incident, the Health and Safety Board suspended Dr. Kenna, pending a full inquiry. Whatever the eventual outcome, the hiatus must surely have ruined her bid for a second round of funding. So we may never find out whether the personal sonar system would have worked outdoors. Dr. Chalmers believes the *Persona* concept was flawed, citing the operational problems posed by the body suit. In his view, Dr. Kenna was as blind as me.

As I ponder this irony, I gradually become aware that the prickling sensation is subsiding. Soon all that remains is a gentle tickling near my belly button. I try to remain calm as the tactile signature ripples over my ribs and up onto my face. Supple fingers stroke my eyes, stimulating muscles that atrophied many months ago. Slowly, my sticky eyelids pull apart, admitting the true darkness at last.

She sits beside me—invisible and untouchable—while I wait for the black to turn to grey.

THE ENGLISH DEAD

The body lay on the North Face of Mount Everest for fifty-one years, its exact location known only to the alpine choughs that pecked at its flesh. Other climbers who attempted the same route were too preoccupied with the hazards of high-altitude mountaineering to conduct a search for their illustrious predecessor.

Then, in the spring of 1975, a Chinese climber stumbled upon the corpse while returning to camp. Wang Hong-bao realised the significance of the dead man's hobnail boots. Only pre-war mountaineers had climbed so high on Everest wearing such primitive gear.

On Wang's return to Everest in 1979, he recounted the incident to a fellow climber. He referred to his find as "The English Dead" but neglected to mention the body's resting place, an omission made permanent two days later by his death in an avalanche.

For twenty years rumours of Wang's discovery circulated in the mountaineering community, provoking fresh interest in one of the enduring mysteries of the Twentieth Century.

"One Hundred Years Ago Today: Did These Men Stand On Top of the World?"
(The Times, June 8 2024)

<< Ben, it's 1400 hours—time you turned back. >>

The voice in Ben's head expressed justifiable concern. Climbing above 8000 metres on Everest was dangerous enough without factoring in the extra risks a solo venture entailed.

<< Don't worry...beginning my descent soon. >>

Ben guessed that his colleagues on the Chomolungma Clean-Up expedition had inferred his objective as soon as he told them he would be descending alone. Scarcely a single Everest climbing season went by without some foolhardy novice making a detour to pay homage to the most revered mountaineer of them all. But Ben was neither a fool nor a novice. Years of meticulous planning had led to this moment, so he proceeded with utmost caution as he traversed the narrow terrace towards the burial mound.

An uncle had given Ben a book on mountaineering for his twelfth birthday. The famous photograph of George Mallory's corpse had provoked a shudder, but also sparked an obsession that deepened with every passing year. Ever since the fatal events of 1924, countless armchair mountaineers had wondered whether Mallory and Irvine reached the summit, twenty-nine years before Edmund Hillary and Tenzing Norgay.

Ben had often imagined the scene: an exhausted but triumphant Mallory holding up a fluttering Union Jack against a backdrop of Himalayan peaks; Irvine's hands shaking as he tried to steady the camera. Dozens of expeditions had searched for Irvine's camera after the discovery of Mallory's body in 1999, but without success. His body, too, had never been found. Ben suspected that Irvine had fallen onto the East Rongbuk glacier, where no corpse would remain visible for long. So rather than undertake another probably futile search, Ben had proposed an innovative new approach to solving the mystery.

<< Ben, it's getting late... >>

<< Five minutes, then I'll start down. >>

Buffeted by the chilling gale-force wind, Ben struggled to undo the clasps on his backpack. Even this apparently simple task made him gasp for breath.

Freed from its container, the seeker squirmed in his hands like a rattlesnake poked with a stick, its sensors responding to the warmth that leaked from his gloves. But on this mission there would be no body-heat for the seeker to home in on; instead, its task was to harvest genetic material from a corpse.

Ben placed the seeker on top of Mallory's burial mound. One flick of its segmented tail and the robot began burrowing into a crevice between two slabs of limestone. Anticipation surged through Ben, erasing any lingering doubts about defiling the grave.

George Leigh Mallory would live again.

Andrew Irvine gazed at the mess of steel cylinders, rubber hoses and regulator valves that littered his tent. Of the dozen sets of oxygen apparatus shipped from Blighty, not one had operated correctly when he'd unpacked the crates. But after several days spent improvising and tinkering, he had cobbled together enough working equipment to support a single attempt on the summit.

Exhilaration gripped Irvine whenever he thought of climbing with Mallory. Even the knowledge that Major Norton had assigned them to the second summit team did nothing to reduce his feelings of anticipation. Howard Somervell and Major Norton, who would make the first attempt, had jokingly dubbed Mallory and Irvine the "Gas Party". In private, he sympathised with those who climbed without oxygen; but as a first-timer on

Everest it was only his expertise with the "English gas", as the Sherpas called it, that had persuaded Mallory to choose him over the expedition's geologist, Noel Odell. So Irvine thanked his lucky stars whenever his comrades made their jibes.

<< Mallory's heading your way, Ben. >>

Odell's interjection jolted Ben out of role. He shook his head in dismay.

<< Odell, you must *never* use my real name! >>

<< Sorry... 'Old habits die hard' and all that. >>

<< I know it's difficult, but we *must* immerse ourselves in our personas rather than rely on technology. >>

<< I know, but... >>

The terms of the contract had made their obligations abundantly clear. Universal's board had insisted on absolute authenticity when they accepted Ben's proposal to restage the 1924 Everest Expedition. Respect for traditional values had also helped soothe away the objections of the Dalai Lama, who a decade earlier had paid handsomely to have his beloved Chomolungma swept clean of Western detritus. Neural recording was supposed to be the expedition's sole concession to modern technology. Head-speak came as a bonus, but Universal had forbidden its use except in emergencies.

<< And Odell... >>

<< Yes? >>

<< You know the rules about head-speak! >>

His comrade's riposte was coarse but good-humoured.

A moment later, an unseen hand pulled open the tent flap. In came the inevitable freezing gust of wind, a swirl of snowflakes—and Mallory. For the first time in a fortnight, that famously handsome though gaunt-looking face wore a grin.

"Great news, Sandy! The weather is clearing. Norton wants us to head up to Camp One. The "Big Push" is on!"

Mallory made the assault on Everest sound like the Battle of the Somme, except here they faced an opponent equipped with avalanches and snowstorms rather than barbed wire and machine-guns. Ben pictured himself struggling up the North Face in the teeth of a howling gale, and immediately slipped back into his Irvine persona.

On a whim, he reached over and ruffled Mallory's crudely barbered hair, turning it into a miniature Himalayas. Mallory responded by slapping him on the back.

"Come on, let's get cracking."

No wonder Mallory looked delighted, thought Irvine. For two weeks, storm-force winds and heavy snow had pounded the mountain, confining the expedition to Base Camp. Mallory had paced back and forth like a caged animal. If the bad weather had persisted for a few more days, dwindling

31

supplies would have forced the expedition to turn back.

Irvine followed Mallory out of the tent. For the first time in a fortnight Base Camp bustled with activity, with Odell taking the lead in marshalling the Sherpas. Bent double under their packs, these sturdy mountain-men resembled beasts of burden.

Aware of the need for urgency, Irvine trotted back to his tent and began packing spare hoses and t-piece connectors. Emerging again with his first load, he spotted Mallory standing aside from the commotion, his gaze fixed on the North Face of Everest. Those dark rock faces, saw-tooth ridges and gleaming snow slopes would present a formidable challenge to the British Empire's finest mountaineer, thought Irvine.

<< Do you suppose Mallory is thinking about 1922? >>

Odell again!

This time Ben refrained from scolding his colleague. In truth, he too had wondered how his climbing partner felt about the disaster that ended the 1922 expedition. Mallory's decision to permit a third summit attempt even as the first snows of the Monsoon began falling had cost seven Sherpas their lives in an avalanche.

<< The neural mapping indicates that Mallory has formed the appropriate memory engrams. >>

<< Even though he didn't actually experience those events? >>

The debate about the fidelity of reconstructions performed by human clones equipped with virtual memories had never entirely subsided, but the demonstrations seen by Ben had convinced him that his project was viable. Universal evidently believed so too. If their fast-tracked clone performed as advertised, then the mystery of Mallory and Irvine would surely be solved. Assuming, of course, that every member of the expedition played his part.

<< Please, Noel. This isn't helping! >>

Odell slapped Ben's shoulder and walked away.

Feeling a sudden itch, Ben peeled back his leather motorcycle helmet and scratched at the stubble that had accumulated on his sunburnt cheeks. If Mallory looked at him now, he would see the boyish features of a twenty-two year-old. But like Mallory, "Sandy" Irvine was not what he seemed.

<< Do you think Mallory will succeed? >>

Ben risked a glance at his climbing partner, who had continued to gaze at the peak while he conversed with Odell. The summit gleamed like a pearl in the morning sunlight, tantalising all those who beheld it with the promise of glory.

<< There's only one way to find out. >>

The time for debate was over.

Having completed his final adjustments to the oxygen apparatus, Irvine looked up to see what Mallory was doing. His climbing partner stood in front of their tiny tent, stamping his hobnail boots and flapping his arms while the canvas billowed in the howling wind. Evidently satisfied with the effect on his circulation, Mallory turned to face the rising sun, as if formally accepting a challenge from a Himalayan deity.

Mallory's lack of urgency worried Irvine. They had already lost precious minutes squeezing their feet into boots as unyielding as granite. For that, Irvine could thank Mallory. Shortly after their arrival at Camp Six, he had allowed their primus stove to slide off the snow terrace. Lacking its meagre warmth, they had been unable to soften their boot-leather or melt snow for a much-needed mug of tea.

Typical bloody George!

Irvine ignored his thirst while he gave the oxygen apparatus a final test. Since arriving at Camp Six, he had spent several hours trying to coax a steady flow of gas from the cylinders. Frozen hoses and leaky connectors were the bane of the hapless engineer obliged to work at 27300 feet.

Hapless but happy, Irvine told himself, as he contemplated the grand adventure that lay ahead. But if their efforts were to be fully rewarded, he would have to persuade Mallory to carry sufficient oxygen. Thus far Irvine had failed to win the argument.

"We could go with three," he said.

Mallory hefted one of the cylinders, puffing out his cheeks as he did so. Then he shook his head.

"Even two would be a bloody load."

Irvine stared at the North East Ridge—a jagged switchback that resembled the armoured plates of a Jurassic dinosaur. According to Mallory, if they could climb the pair of "steps" that jutted out from the ridge they would have a fair chance of reaching the summit. But to overcome such formidable obstacles they would need plenty of time and oxygen. Now it seemed they would be short of both.

"But shouldn't we carry as much oxygen as possible?"

Mallory shook his head again. "No, three cylinders is too heavy a burden. We'll go with two."

Irvine felt a pang of disappointment but tried to mask his feelings with an eager grin.

"A quick dash to the summit!"

"That's the spirit."

Irvine looked on in dismay as Mallory discarded sundry items of mountaineering equipment: a spare coil of rope, flares, even a lantern. There would be little hope for them if they became lost on the North Face in fading light.

There was, however, one item of equipment that Mallory dared not discard. If Everest surrendered to his indomitable will, Irvine planned to record the moment for posterity using Somervell's Kodak camera. The surprisingly small device fitted snugly in the pocket of his Shackleton jacket.

<< How many oxygen cylinders is Mallory carrying? >>

Furious at having been jolted from his role again, Ben cursed Odell. The geologist's desire for updates was proving hugely unhelpful.

<< Just the two. >>

<< Then he stands no chance. >>

The argument had raged for more than a century, but the consensus was that if Mallory had climbed with only two cylinders he stood little chance of reaching the summit. Ben tried to mask his own sense of disappointment when he responded to Odell.

<< We shall see. >>

<< We won't, but you will! >>

<< My neural implant will record the climb. But please, no more contact from now on. You know the rules! >>

It took no effort at all for Ben to reassume his Irvine persona. Sweeping his gaze up the North Face evoked the necessary awe.

Irvine turned to Mallory, who was struggling to don his oxygen apparatus. With mask dangling and gas hose looped and kinked, Mallory resembled Irvine's science master at Shrewsbury Public School. Both men were capable of a hangdog expression that made him chuckle.

"Here—let me help you with that."

Mallory frowned at him.

"Sandy, we are about to embark on the most hazardous adventure of our lives. There will be no time for laughter or debate." Mallory drew a deep, ragged breath before continuing. "But do exactly as I tell you...and we shall stand on the top of the world." He glanced at his watch. "It's time we were off."

Linked to his partner by a hemp rope of questionable strength and carrying a "bloody load" of oxygen, Irvine began clambering over the ice-covered slabs that would lead them into the Yellow Band—the easiest, yet still treacherous, section of their climb.

Within minutes he was shivering like a victim of Malaria.

The oxygen mask plucked at Irvine's sunburnt skin as he pulled it away from his face, making him wince. Half-a-dozen yards further up the slope, Mallory leaned against a limestone outcrop, gasping for breath. Unlike Irvine he had not quite exhausted his first cylinder.

Handicapped by fingers that could barely flex inside two pairs of gloves, Irvine struggled to ease the empty cylinder from its clips. To make matters worse, when he finally managed to engage the second cylinder the renewed flow of gas rasped his throat like sandpaper, making him cough.

THE ENGLISH DEAD

Dispirited, Irvine glanced up at the gleaming summit pyramid, which seemed to pulse in synchrony with the throb in his head.

"Looks a long way," he said.

Mallory grimaced. "We must crack on!"

Irvine knew better than to argue. After nearly four hours of relatively easy climbing, they had reached the base of the First Step. Viewed close-up, the rock-face looked less imposing than he'd expected. Even so, Mallory's decision to traverse around it had come as a relief.

"Could we do...the same thing...at the Second Step?"

Viewed from Camp Six that morning, the higher of the two main obstacles along Mallory's proposed route had seemed to jut out from the North East Ridge like the bows of a battleship. To Irvine, it looked unclimbable.

"Did that work...for Norton?"

"No, but..."

Mallory's snort of derision silenced Irvine. Norton's solo traverse across the North Face towards the huge snow gully known as the Great Couloir had set a new altitude record but failed to open up an alternative route to the summit. Irvine admired the man for his bravery and determination, though not for temporarily abandoning the exhausted Somervell.

"It will be quicker...if we make a traverse...here," gasped Mallory. "Then we climb the ridge."

Irvine nodded. If anyone could find a way up the Second Step it was Mallory. The man had earned his reputation by tackling daunting ridge climbs.

Halfway through the traverse, Mallory changed over to his second cylinder. When the Second Step came into view again, Irvine shook his head, despairing of the task that confronted them. Mallory, on the other hand, seemed to find inspiration in the formidable outcrop of grey limestone.

"Come on Sandy, one more big push!"

Irvine groaned inwardly. By his reckoning they had climbed one third of the vertical distance from Camp Six to the summit. And in doing so, they had consumed half of their oxygen. He tried to shake off the mental image of the cylinders they had left behind.

That the remainder of their summit attempt would be considerably more testing became clear to Irvine when he began inching along the ridge. Buffeted by the worsening gale, he struggled to focus on the bent-double figure of Mallory, a dozen yards ahead. But it was the sheer drop to either side that dominated his thoughts. Eventually, the urge to look down overwhelmed his willpower. The serried ranks of Himalayan peaks seemed to revolve in a stately dance, making his head swim. He closed his eyes, seeking temporary relief in darkness.

The tug of the rope brought him back from the brink. Comforted by Mallory's presence, he shuffled forwards another step.

Still trembling from his ordeal on the ridge, Irvine sought shelter from the gale while Mallory inspected the final pitch of the Second Step. The rock-face constituted a climber's nightmare: a vertical wall of rotten, crumbling limestone. To free-climb it at sea level would have been have been a stern enough test of Mallory's skill. As for making the attempt at altitude while burdened with oxygen apparatus, that seemed too much to expect of any climber, even Mallory.

Irvine glanced at his altimeter. The needle indicated 28300 feet, proof that they had climbed higher than Norton. Would Mallory regard a new altitude record as a worthwhile achievement? It seemed unlikely.

Mallory removed his oxygen mask and glanced at his watch. "Ten to one," he said in a tone that betrayed no particular concern.

Hearing those words made Ben shudder, though at first he struggled to understand why. The cause of his disquiet only became clear when he realised that he had slipped out of role.

Ten minutes to one o'clock!

Noel Odell had observed Mallory and Irvine ascending the North East Ridge at precisely that time on June 8th, 1924. Some experts dismissed the sighting as a mirage, others disputed the precise location on the ridge, but Ben had never doubted that the keen-sighted geologist had spotted the second summit party. If everything were going to plan, *his* Odell would be repeating that observation right now.

Would history repeat itself in other ways too?

Everything depended on how Mallory judged the situation. Would he risk all for a faint chance of glory? With little more than an hour's worth of oxygen remaining, Ben knew that making a safe descent to Camp Six during daylight would prove a stern test for two tired climbers. But if Mallory climbed the Second Step and pushed on towards the summit, their descent would take place in darkness. Exposed to Arctic temperatures and with no flares or lantern to illuminate their way, the odds would not favour survival.

But that, surely, was the point of the re-enactment. He had climbed this high on Everest to find out what the original Mallory would have done when confronted with the same situation.

Aware that if "Irvine" acted out of character it would bias the re-enactment, Ben forced himself to re-adopt his persona.

"One last big push, eh?"

Mallory slapped Irvine on the shoulder. "That's the spirit!"

Moments after resuming his search for a route up the rock-face, Mallory let out a whoop. He was grinning like a child in a sweetshop.

"Look at this crack," he said, gesticulating at the rock-face. "I think it will 'go'!"

Irvine examined the fissure, which seemed to penetrate deep into the rock. If it extended all the way to the top, there might be a chance of reaching the summit!

"We've come all this way," he gasped. "Be a pity..."

"Good man!"

Irvine looked on with admiration as Mallory tackled the climb. His method was typically unorthodox. He began by sliding his left knee up the fissure until he had it wedged in securely. Next he reached upwards, his body pivoting around his knee, while he scrabbled for handholds. Finally Mallory found what he needed and hauled himself several feet up the cliff-face. Then he set about repeating the procedure.

A powerful gust brought with it the first snow flurry of the day. Irvine hunkered down at the base of the cliff with his back to the wind, paying out rope an arm's length at a time while waiting for Mallory's call. If he reached the top, Irvine would have to follow his partner.

For several minutes the only sound Irvine heard over the gale was the scratching of hobnails against limestone. Then he realised that the rope had stopped tugging. Despair filled Irvine's heart as he watched his partner descend amidst a shower of rock fragments.

Mallory jumped down the last few feet, but landed awkwardly and fell onto his back. As Irvine pulled him upright, he asked, "Won't it 'go'?"

He had expected a show of frustration or dismay from his partner, but not a fit of rage, which culminated in Mallory hurling his oxygen apparatus against the rock-face, damaging it beyond hope of repair.

"Oh it will 'go' all right," yelled Mallory. "But someone has *gone* there before me!" He waved the shaft of a metal bolt beneath Irvine's nose. "Worse, he *cheated*!"

Irvine peered at the cliff-face, bewildered. No one had climbed this high on Everest before, so how could...?

Imagined scenes from successful ascents of the Second Step formed in his mind. Too late, Ben realised that he had slipped out of role again.

First there had been the Chinese expedition of 1960, whose climbers stood on each other's shoulders to surmount the obstacle. Then, fifteen years later, members of the second Chinese expedition fastened an aluminium ladder to the rock-face, making a hitherto impassable route almost straightforward.

Hundreds of climbers used the Chinese ladder and its successors until, in 2064, the Dalai Lama's expedition began removing the debris left by fourteen decades of mountaineering. Ben recalled watching a party of Sherpas carry the last of the ladders back down to Base Camp. The expedition's geologist had declared that the pressure exerted by surrounding rock would compact the drill-holes. Eventually there would be no trace at all; assuming, of course, that the Sherpas had removed the bolts, not just sliced through them...

The devil was in the detail, as always.

Ben turned to face his partner, arms spread wide in a gesture of contrition. Mallory shoved him aside, his expression so ferocious it threatened to reduce the world's highest mountain to rubble.

Unable to see more than a few yards in any direction, Ben had begun to fixate on the tug of the rope, the only tangible evidence that Mallory had not deserted him.

After the debacle at the Second Step, Mallory's flawless mountain-craft had brought them safely down the ridge, but the snow flurries had merged into a whiteout as they traversed around the First Step. Now, Ben and his disillusioned partner were lost somewhere in the Yellow Band.

Ben had considered calling for help, but even if Odell could persuade the others to flout expedition rules and attempt a rescue, he doubted that they would make much progress in such atrocious conditions.

Not that Ben gave a damn about historical accuracy any more. All pretence had been abandoned at the Second Step, likewise any semblance of trust. Even Mallory felt able to break the rules now: leading the descent when standard practice dictated that the less experienced climber should go first.

Ben had compounded his crime by dropping his ice axe just below the First Step. Befuddled by lack of oxygen, he had clambered down the snow-covered slabs for several minutes before realising what he had done. After enduring Mallory's wrath, he remembered that a member of the 1933 expedition had found Irvine's ice axe near the First Step. History seemed determined to repeat itself whether Ben played the game or not.

Sheltering from the gale near the top of a narrow gully, Ben peered through the snowflakes, which he noticed were falling less heavily now. He could just make out Mallory standing at the bottom, taking a breather. Though tempted to hurry down the easy-looking slope, Ben knew better than to take the risk. In any case, one laboured step for every five breaths was the best he could manage.

Ben closed to within touching distance before he noticed Mallory's lips moving. A painful-sounding gasp followed each trickle of words.

"Mapped a route...in '21... First summit attempt...in '22... No other expeditions!" Mallory shook his head, as if doubting his own memories. "No one...could have climbed...the Second Step...before me!"

A glimpse of Mallory's tormented expression convinced Ben that he deserved to know the truth.

"George...this isn't...1924."

"Not 1924?" Mallory gawped at him. "Ridiculous!"

Now it was Ben's turn to shake his head. "Hundred and fifty years ago...Mallory and Irvine...died during...descent." He paused for a moment, his chest heaving. "I wanted to know... Did they...summit?"

He let Mallory work through the implications.

"Then who...am I?"

"A replica...the best...science could make."

That moment of confession, so long delayed, brought with it a powerful feeling of release. Exhaustion swept over Ben like an avalanche. His eyes closed as he keeled over. If he could just rest here for a few seconds, he would be fine. He began counting.

One, two, three...four...

A jerk of the rope brought him back from the brink. With a sigh as vast as Everest, Ben opened his eyes. Another jerk pulled him into a sitting position. Then Mallory placed his hands under his armpits and tugged him upright.

"Come on Sandy... One last big push."

Mallory's change of heart proved to be just the spur Ben required. For a while he dared to hope that they might make it back to Camp Six, until the storm clouds pulled back across the North Face, revealing just how far they had strayed off course. But if they had misjudged their path so badly, why did the vista provoke such a powerful feeling of déjà vu?

Worried that he might be hallucinating, Ben looked down the scree slope towards Mallory, hoping for reassurance. His partner stood on a narrow snow terrace, staring up at the North East Ridge, as if committing their descent to memory. To Ben, this seemed a perverse thing to do given their perilous situation. Several minutes of lung-bursting effort brought him level with Mallory, who obligingly gasped out an explanation.

"Sandy...if we'd fallen...where you dropped...your ice axe...we'd have come to rest...'bout here."

Realisation came suddenly to Ben. He knew this place. He had stood here before!

<< Ben, we've spotted you! >>

He let his gaze slide along the terrace until he caught sight of the snow-covered mound, situated less than thirty metres away.

<< Ben, I'm moving up from Camp Six with a team of Sherpas. We should reach you in an hour, maybe less. >>

Mallory plucked at his sleeve, dragging his attention away from the strange voice in his head. He waved a trembling arm towards the mound.

"Is this...the place?"

Ben could find no words, managed only the most sluggish of nods. But that was enough to start Mallory on a painstaking traverse of the terrace.

<< Ben, did Mallory reach the summit? >>

Who was this Ben person anyway? Had Mallory decided to climb with someone else?

<< Ben, did Mallory climb the Second Step? >>

Rather than converse with his phantom interrogator, who sounded like some insufferable Alpine Club grandee, Irvine fixed his gaze on the man he revered, but exhaustion made his head drop. The third time he looked up, he saw Mallory standing by the mound. A Union Jack fluttered in his hands.

"Sandy...would you take...a picture?"

<< Ben, you must talk to me! >>

Summoning his last reserves of energy, Irvine pulled the camera from his pocket and pointed it at his partner.

Framed against the darkening sky, Mallory looked down upon the lesser peaks as if he were a god.

As he watched his colleagues take down the tents, Ben realised that this was the first day since his rescue that no one had asked him whether Mallory reached the summit. That presumably meant that Odell and co had decoded the sensory recordings from his neural implant. No doubt they were disappointed. So, too, would be Universal. Still, if the board gave the go-ahead, the 1924 scenario could be repeated until they obtained the outcome that Ben had dreamt of since childhood. Just tidy up the Second Step, clone another Mallory, fake another Irvine. Easy.

"What happened to the camera?"

Ben had prepared an answer for that question, too.

Lost on Everest, same as Mallory.

When the rescue party found Ben, he had been lying face down on the snow terrace, mumbling Mallory's name. The last thing he recalled was that the rope no longer tugged at his waist. Despite a frantic search, Odell and the Sherpas found no sign of Mallory or the camera.

Ben liked to think that he had hurled the camera into the void in a last-ditch attempt to renew the mystery. More likely, Mallory had taken it from him after he lapsed into semi-consciousness. He also liked to think that when Mallory spotted their rescuers climbing towards them, the great man had turned around and started back up the mountain.

With his face warmed by the rising sun, Ben contemplated the summit for what he knew would be the last time. He offered up a prayer to the great Chomolungma, in the hope that any future Irvine would succeed in persuading Mallory to carry a third oxygen cylinder.

STARS IN HER EYES

Jerome Dalton gazed at an October night-sky made perfect by the absence of moonlight. Arching overhead, the Milky Way resembled a strip of gauze draped over black velvet. Having set up his CCD-equipped Celestron so that it tracked the Andromeda Galaxy, Jerome fully intended to indulge his passion for stargazing.

The sound of footfalls startled him. Before he could step aside, a thump in the back tumbled him to the ground. Winded, he stared up at his assailant, who was sliding a bulky pair of headphones off her ears.

"Shit! Sorry, I didn't see you..." The woman's apology dribbled away into the air.

Jerome pushed her hands away. "I can manage," he grumbled. Upright again, he unclipped his torch and thumbed it on. He felt no remorse at ruining the woman's night vision.

"Sorry, that was so my fault," she said, blinking.

Seeing her remorseful expression, Jerome softened his tone. "Well, you missed the 'scope, that's the main thing."

A smile led to a handshake and an exchange of names.

Lenora Kelly stood chin-high to him, five-three or thereabouts. Jet-black hair bobbed a la mode framed prominent cheekbones and a ski-jump nose. Stargazer-standard fleece and baggy pants hid her presumably skinny physique. Quite good-looking in a quirky kind of way, he decided, surprised that he hadn't noticed her before. Dozens of amateur astronomers had pitched their tents around Patterson Lake, tempted out of Greater Seattle by a rare forecast of fine weather. Most of them were male.

"What're you listening to?"

She passed him the headphones. "Here, give it a try."

After a brief inspection of the headband, which incorporated a stubby antenna, he placed the 'phones over his ears. He heard a faint, burbling hiss. He tilted his head. The sound grew louder as the Milky Way came into view, faded as his gaze skated past. Unimpressed by this simple modulation of celestial static, he handed the 'phones back to Lenora. Her smile flared to nova strength.

"Wonderful, isn't it?"

Faced with that smile, he wished he could agree, but five years of marriage had shown him that telling lies was not his forte.

"Wouldn't want to listen to the 21-cm hydrogen line all night long."

Seemingly undeterred by his indifference, she tapped the antenna. "This connects to the SETI Institute's all-sky database, so I get to listen to the freshest data from wherever I'm looking. Head-tracked radio astronomy—cool, huh?"

Jerome chuckled at her mention of SETI. "I signed up for SETI@home back in the late Nineties! Then I lost my job at Boeing, so I had to find more lucrative ways to exploit my computer's idle time." And latterly his own, of course.

Lenora shrugged like someone hearing a familiar story.

Fearing her interest was waning, Jerome pointed towards the zenith, "Reckon there's anyone on the phone?"

"Has to be," she whispered.

"But why do you listen?"

She shrugged. "I like to be involved."

Her answer sounded self-deluding to Jerome, but he kept the thought to himself. Better to have a specious purpose in life than none at all, which pretty much described his own situation since Josie packed her bags.

After failing to stifle a yawn, he pointed his torch at his 'scope. "I'm going to download the image and then crash for the night." The idea of zipping together two sleeping bags flashed into his mind like a meteor but expired just as quickly.

You've got ten years on her!

To his surprise, Lenora remained with him while he booted up his laptop. As he'd half-expected, the Andromeda image had tanked. Not wishing her to see him so easily thwarted, he loaded the file into a picture enhancement application a lecturer friend at UCLA had copied for him.

"I'll let that brew overnight."

Lenora hunkered down beside him. "You could get involved too," she whispered.

"How do you mean?"

She gave him an appraising look. "Did you bring your WhileAway console?"

How had she worked that out? Mind you, Josie had reckoned he looked the sort.

"I figured if someone had brought their server I could hook up and earn ten dollars."

Did that make him sound like a tightwad?

To his relief, Lenora lit another smile. "Well, luckily for you, my partner did bring his server." She winkled a thumb-drive out of her pocket. "And if you'd like to try something different, just load this patch and then…"

"And then what, exactly?" he asked, irritated by her reference to a partner, concerned too that he might be falling for a scam. Rumours of WhileAway hackers abounded in the blogosphere.

"And then I'll see you tomorrow for breakfast."

The alternative of subsisting on cereal bars made her invitation seem enticing.

"That's my tent over there," said Lenora, pointing along the path. Jerome wished her goodnight as she turned away.

After packing away his 'scope, Jerome loaded Lenora's patch onto his WhileAway console. Satisfied, he donned his skullcap and snuggled down in his sleeping bag. He tried to ignore the prickle of electrodes against his scalp while he waited for sleep to come.

The setting sun twitched ribbons of crimson between gunmetal waves. A salt-tangy breeze ruffled his hair. Surf sluiced over his feet, making him shiver as he strolled the infinite beach.

Aware he was supposed to be looking for something, he squatted down at the water's edge and began sifting through flotsam. He pushed aside a plank of driftwood and found a piece of glass.

Something made of glass; he was searching for something made of glass.

Beaches…he hated beaches… Body not toned enough…

But beachcombing… That was fun!

Jerome stretched out his arms and plucked the skullcap from his head. For once he didn't feel woozy from having his REM sleep messed about by WhileAway. Usually he dreamt of searching for a needle in a haystack, the standard metaphor used by biotech companies that rented his downtime. Beachcombing certainly had that beat.

Recalling Lenora's offer of breakfast, Jerome unzipped his sleeping bag. As he wriggled free, he heard someone moving outside the tent. Before he could call out, a hand tugged at the flap. A face previously seen by torchlight peered in.

"So how was it for you?"

"Pretty cool," Jerome replied, his voice not quite masking the rumbling from his stomach. "Any chance of breakfast?"

"Might manage a coffee."

Jerome pulled on his Levis and shirt and followed Lenora outside. A short walk along the lakeside brought them to her tent. Big enough for two, he observed. Lenora pulled open the flap.

"Who have you got there?" said a male voice. "Another recruit?"

Lenora arched a neatly plucked eyebrow. "Maybe."

The man who emerged wore calf-length cargo pants and a black tee shirt that showed off his biceps. Sporting a wispy beard and mane of straw-coloured hair, he looked more surfer-dude than WhileAway geek. Older than Lenora, Jerome surmised.

She introduced him to Zane, who ignored Jerome's proffered hand. "Is he staying here tonight?"

Jerome scanned the lakeside. Most of the astronomers had already departed, but he felt no desire to follow them. Camping weekends were as much vacation as his income allowed.

He glanced at Lenora. "Well, last night's dream was kind of fun."

"You've got Zane to thank for that."

Jerome turned towards him. "So, what's your cut?"

Zane's eyes flicked skywards. "WhileAway would sue our hides if they knew what we're up to. So no, SETI dreaming won't earn you a dime, never mind ten bucks."

"No problem. The dream was worth the money, easy."

Lenora nailed him with another of her smiles. Zane gave him a pitying look and ducked back into the tent.

Lenora squeezed Jerome's arm. "Last night was just a taster. The next dream will be a lot more fun."

Despite Lenora's show of affection, Jerome couldn't quite convince himself she really wanted him. Still, if he followed her lead, who knew where he might end up? Better still, he could take the lead.

Over coffee, he suggested a walk around the lake. He enjoyed watching Zane's expression turn even sourer when Lenora told him.

"He's just being boorish," she said, when safely out of earshot. "We were lovers once, years ago. Now we're just partners in crime."

This encouraging news was pretty much all Jerome learnt about Lenora while they walked around the lake. He answered several questions regarding life with Josie, whereas she deflected his with aplomb. When he asked about her job, she flashed her lovely smile and changed the subject. No less mysterious was her decision to carry a backpack on a walk that seemed likely to last no more than two hours. He was about to suggest that he take it for a while when she flopped down on a boulder that jutted into the lake.

"Room for two," she said, patting the rock.

Smiling, he sat down next to her and removed his boots. He dangled his feet in the water. The cold made him flinch, but the warmth of the sunlight compensated nicely. He lay back, luxuriating in the feeling that all was right with the world.

"Close your eyes."

He obeyed, hoping for a kiss. Instead Lenora's breath tickled his ear. "And keep them closed!"

He heard rummaging sounds. Moments later, he felt electrodes prickle against his scalp. On opening his eyes he saw that Lenora was also wearing a WhileAway cap.

"Are you sure we'll receive a signal here?"

She held up two consoles. Both readouts showed five green bars.

"Okay, but I don't feel sleepy."

She rattled a bottle and shook out two pink pills. "These babies will see to that."

Jerome felt tempted to suggest a more enjoyable way, but his courage deserted him. Seeing his doleful expression, Lenora leaned over and kissed him on the lips.

"A little bodily contact helps promote shared dreaming, but too much gets in the way." She winked at him. "Just give me a minute."

After configuring the WhileAway consoles for synchronous operation, Lenora clambered back onto the boulder. She lay beside Jerome with knees slightly raised, her bare forearm touching his.

There were, he mused, much worse ways to spend an afternoon.

Strolling hand in hand along the infinite beach, he felt as though he could walk forever.

Too soon, his partner tugged her hand free and fell to her knees. He hunkered down beside her and began sifting shingle.

What are we looking for?

A bottle, silly; a message in a bottle!

Ah, yes! Something made of glass.

Their search turned up not so much as a fragment, let alone a bottle. Unconcerned, he skimmed pebbles beyond the breaking waves.

Laughing, they resumed their walk in the sun.

Jerome blinked until the grey blobs came into focus. Cumulonimbus clouds towered over Lake Patterson. A glance at his wristwatch revealed three hours had passed.

"Did you enjoy the dream?" asked Lenora.

"Yeah, that was fun," he replied, "if frustrating." Seeing her expression, he added: "Not finding a bottle, I mean."

"SETI dreamers must be patient."

"Pity the weather gods haven't mastered that trick," he said, glancing at the sky.

They jogged back to the camp, taking turns with the backpack, but the storm won the race. Hailstones pelted them as they sprinted the last hundred yards.

"See you tonight at the beach!" Lenora yelled as she ducked into her tent.

Jerome stripped off and towelled himself dry. Aware that he hadn't brought a change of clothes, he considered jumping into his pickup truck and driving off. But Lenora's exhortation held him back.

He spent the evening reading a paperback novel by torchlight. When the storm finally rumbled off into the Cascades, he switched on his WhileAway console, selected auto-synch and reached for his cap.

Annoyed that she had let go of his hand again, he flopped down in the shallows. The ebb and flow tugged at him while he waited for her to finish examining whatever had caught her eye.

Looking to his left, he spied a man standing on a distant sand dune. The man seemed familiar but did not respond to his wave.

A triumphant yell startled him into sitting up. He stared at his partner. She was holding a bottle aloft, her trophy gleaming in the sunlight. He leapt to his feet, but the sand sucked at his heels, turning his sprint into a moonwalk. As he reached out towards her she faded from view. The bottle thudded onto sand; a sheet of paper wafted nearby.

No longer bogged down, he snatched up the paper before the breeze could blow it into the sea. He held the sheet at arm's length. Frowning, he turned it over.

Blank on both sides.

Jerome woke to the sound of rain pummelling his tent. Forked lightning zigzagged through the darkness; thunder rumbled like tympani. He wriggled deeper into his sleeping bag, fingertips jammed in his ears. Even with his eyes shut tight he could still see the lightning.

A sudden inrush of air made the tent billow alarmingly. Jerome opened his eyes and saw Zane's head poke through the flap.

"Quick, get your waterproofs on," Zane yelled. "Lenora's gone missing!"

"What the hell is she...?"

Zane backed out before Jerome could finish his question. He wriggled into his sodden Levis, tugged on his boots and jacket. Outside he found Zane jogging along the lakeside, hair plastered over his face, shouting "Lenora!"

Jerome shielded his eyes with both hands while he scanned the landscape. Lightning lit up the nearest hill just long enough for him to glimpse a figure standing at the summit.

"She's up there!" he shouted, pointing at the hill.

Trusting that Zane would follow him, Jerome charged up the slope. He weaved past Douglas Firs and tangles of bitterbrush, heedless of the danger from lightning.

On reaching the summit he paused for a moment to catch his breath. What he saw there made his jaw drop. Not twenty yards away Lenora danced naked beneath the lashing rain. She had just skipped to a fist-sized stone and was now turning on the spot, her feet shuffling either side of the marker. After completing three spins, she skipped over to another stone and repeated the sequence. Jerome counted a dozen such moves before Lenora stooped to pick up her markers. After placing them in a new pattern, she resumed her dance, oblivious to the rain or her audience.

An ear-splitting crash reminded Jerome of the urgent need to get off the hilltop. He stripped off his jacket and moved in on Lenora, timing his lunge so he caught her off balance. He snared her left arm and yanked it behind her back, hoping to restrain her, but she squirmed like an eel.

"Zane, I need some help here!"

Zane rushed forward and grabbed Lenora's free arm. Working together, they managed to pull the jacket over her trembling shoulders. Lenora wriggled and jerked, her head darting left and right as if she were memorising the positions of the stones. The patterns did seem vaguely familiar to Jerome. Over there, wasn't that a "W"?

He pushed the thought to the back of his mind.

Zane led the way downhill. Halfway to the camp, Lenora tripped herself, sending Jerome tumbling into a bush. Bleeding from cuts to his hands and face, he extricated himself while Zane struggled to restrain Lenora. By the time they reached the lake, she had lapsed into unconsciousness.

Jerome unzipped the flap to Lenora's tent and held it open while Zane bundled her inside. When Jerome tried to follow he found his way blocked. Unwilling to leave until reassured about Lenora's condition, he waited outside in the rain. He had just shouted his third offer of help when Zane pushed through the flap.

"Leave this to me. I know what I'm doing."

Jerome gaped at him. "Lenora is having a fit! She needs to be in a hospital. If you're too scared to take her there, I'll do it!"

Zane stood facing Jerome, hands planted on hips.

"Strictly speaking, Lenora has had a fit. Now it's over, she'll be unconscious for several hours. I know what to do, so let me look after her, okay?"

Unwilling to be fobbed off, Jerome tried to push past Zane, who responded with a two-handed shove. Jerome landed hard in a puddle.

Zane looked mortified. "Look, I'm sorry, I didn't mean to…"

Jerome cuffed away his helping hand. "If Lenora comes to any harm, I'm holding you responsible! You got that?"

Zane made a placating gesture. "Trust me, Lenora will be fine. But if it makes you feel better, I'll drive her to hospital, soon as it's safe."

Jerome climbed to his feet. In truth, he felt too exhausted to drive, even though the rain had slackened off a bit and the thunder now trailed the lightning by several seconds.

"Storm's heading off," he muttered, inclining his head towards Zane's SUV.

Zane held up both hands. "Okay, okay."

Jerome helped Zane strap Lenora into a rear seat, but when he strode round to the passenger door, he found it locked.

"For pity's sake!" yelled Zane, eyes blazing, "Go dry yourself off and get some sleep. Otherwise you'll be no help to Lenora tomorrow."

Pondering Zane's last remark kept Jerome awake long after the thunder had rumbled into the distance.

Turn, turn, turn and skip; turn, turn, turn and skip: dance to the pattern of the stars...

Jerome plucked at his scalp while blinking away the dregs of the dream, but didn't find the expected skullcap. Evidently his subconscious had stimulated that last dream, unlike its predecessor.

Reluctant to leave the warmth of his sleeping bag, Jerome thought about what he'd witnessed on the hilltop and the dream that preceded it. Lenora's dancing must be her way of interpreting alien messages, he realised. The implication was astonishing. Lenora had made First Contact!

But at what cost to her health?

The growl of an engine revving in low gear made Jerome start. He tugged on his jeans and crawled outside, expecting to find Zane parking his SUV. Instead, he observed a convoy rumbling up the gravel road. Lenora stood on the lakeside path, waving to each driver in turn; a queenly gesture.

Jerome counted eleven vehicles, each driven by an unaccompanied man. Was that all he meant to Lenora? Merely a convenient way to boost her recruits to a symbolically pleasing dozen!

Lenora arched an eyebrow as he approached. "See you tonight," she said, before turning smartly. The set of her shoulders suggested pursuit would not be tolerated.

He'd have to confront Zane instead.

Jerome found Zane unpacking a dish antenna from a wooden crate. A radio station blared from Zane's laptop. Space Oddity had just segued into Starman.

"So it really is happening," said Jerome.

"Yeah, you just missed the news conference."

"What's the low-down?"

"Six months ago, one of NASA's satellites detected a sustained burst of gamma rays from an object previously classified as a comet. Having changed course for Earth, the unidentified spacecraft began transmitting signals. Problem was, NASA's experts couldn't interpret them. They still can't."

"But Lenora can."

"Correct."

Jerome pointed at the antenna. "What's this for, then?"

"Back-up in case the SETI feed goes off-line before the spacecraft reaches Earth, forty-eight hours from now."

"Bit late for the President to pull the plug, surely?"

"Can't take the risk, not when Lenora's this close to success." Zane pressed thumb and forefinger together.

"If she's that close, why does she need these guys?" asked Jerome, pointing towards the nearest tent. "Or me, for that matter."

Zane rolled his eyes. "Do I really have to explain Lenora's modus operandi?"

"I figured that out for myself, thanks," Jerome replied. "The patterns Lenora danced last night depicted the stars as seen from a planet en route to Earth. A celestial postcard, if you like."

"Yeah, dancing is the key," said Zane. "And if Lenora only had to read one message tonight, she'd be okay. But as the spacecraft nears Earth, the signal bandwidth will increase dramatically. So Lenora will have to read a lot of messages very quickly. To do that, she needs help. Which is where you come in."

A collective dream reading did make a weird kind of sense, thought Jerome. But had Zane considered the consequences? He swept his arm, indicating the entire campsite.

"So Zane, have you booked enough ambulances for tomorrow? Because from what I saw last night, every one of Lenora's disciples will need several hours of treatment."

"I've got a team of helpers on stand-by," Zane said, matter-of-factly. "So, if that's all, I've got a deadline to meet." He strode towards the nearest tent. Unwilling to be fobbed off, Jerome followed him inside.

On seeing Zane, the tent's occupant wrinkled his nose as if he'd detected a bad smell. For a moment, it seemed a single word might spark a fight; then Zane shrugged and turned away. After adjusting the man's WhileAway console, he tapped two pink pills into his upturned palm.

Outside again, Jerome asked, "What was that all about?"

"He's Number Two."

"Meaning what, exactly?"

"Well, you're Number Thirteen."

The implication became clear to Jerome.

"So you were Lenora's first?"

"Yeah," said Zane. "And believe me, with Lenora first was definitely worst." He chuckled mirthlessly. "So now, as penance, I get to build a supercomputer out of her ex-boyfriends."

Jerome sympathised with Zane's plight, but Lenora's plan for her disciples concerned him much more. Keen to exploit Zane's confessional state of mind, he asked how he knew her.

"We met at Caltech while I was studying for a Ph.D.," Zane recounted. "We fell in love, which was great; then she fell out of love, which wasn't. But we remained friends.

"After Lenora graduated, WhileAway recruited her to work on dream metaphors, whereas I drifted into white hacking." Jerome raised his eyebrows, prompting a grin from Zane. "Corporations pay well to have their security tested.

"Anyhow, Lenora had seen off four more boyfriends when she asked me to hack into the SETI Institute's database. I jumped at the chance, thinking it might get me back into her good books." He glanced at Jerome. "Did you try her SETI radio?"

"Yeah, that's how she hooked me."

Zane winced. "So, having successfully exploited my infatuation, she explained her idea for detecting signals from alien civilisations. No chance, I reckoned. But nine months after her first SETI dream, she found a bottle. Reading its message put her in an ICU for two weeks. Yet she tried again. Last night was her fifth message. Fortunately, she recovers a lot quicker now."

Jerome grabbed Zane by both shoulders, appalled by the implication.

"For God's sake man, Lenora's plan is outrageous! Sure, she'll recover in time to watch CNN broadcast the landing, but what about her disciples? They'll endure brainstorms lasting for weeks! How can you consider inflicting such suffering on them?"

Zane shrugged. "Someone's gotta do the Beta testing."

A suspicion was growing in Jerome's mind.

"What, precisely, do you have planned for tomorrow night?"

Zane's eyes gleamed with a prophet's fervour. "If tonight's dry-run is successful, I'll be networking ten thousand sleeping minds into a SETI dream."

Jerome shook his head in dismay. Zane's unrequited love had made things so easy for Lenora. He had thrown himself into her scheme with no thought of the consequences. Yet something must be bothering him, because he was standing there wringing his hands. Jerome decided that an appeal to geek vanity might reveal a weakness he could exploit.

"So how does it work?"

Zane's eyes lit up again. "I've infected the entire WhileAway network with a stealthed virus that will reprogram the metaphor generator of every user who's also registered with SETI@home."

"The ultimate love bug, eh?"

Zane's mouth twitched into a grin.

"Can you neutralise the virus?"

Zane snorted. "Viruses don't have off switches!"

"What about WhileAway's own defences?"

"Their network antibodies won't stop this virus."

"But surely if I told them Lenora's plan, WhileAway would take the service off-line."

"It would be your word against hers. Who do you think they'd believe?"

Not that WhileAway, or anyone else, would pay attention to his accusation while Humanity stood on the brink of such an historic event.

Zane pushed past him. "I'm still working to that deadline."

Dismayed by his inability to influence Zane, Jerome plodded down to the lake. A Mallard duck waddled past him, quacking for easy pickings. Right now, communicating with wildfowl seemed a lot easier than trying to get through to Zane. Even talking to aliens couldn't be this difficult!

But that was it, Jerome realised. We should be talking to them not just listening. How else could humankind hope to achieve genuine understanding? He jogged back to the camp, found Zane inside his tent and frogmarched him to the antenna.

"What if we used this thing to send a message from within a dream?" said Jerome. "If we could persuade the aliens to only transmit isolated, simple messages, Lenora could manage without helpers."

Zane gave a fierce shake of his head.

"If you think I'm..."

Jerome grabbed his shoulders and shook him. "If Lenora gets her way, thousands will suffer! For God's sake man, you absolutely have to think!"

Zane lowered his gaze but said nothing.

"My friend, Lenora won't ever take you back."

Zane gave a long sigh. "I know."

"So will you help me put a stop to this madness?"

After a pause, Zane nodded. Then his expression went blank, as if he had focussed his mind's eye on some internal computer screen. Several minutes passed before he replied.

"From a purely technical standpoint, it's do-able. I can modulate your brainwaves over the WhileAway carrier and push out the signal on the aliens' frequency." He paused, frowning. "But how will you compose a message they'll understand? You can't just write 'turn down the volume' in English!"

Jerome gestured frantically. "Dammit Zane, they build spaceships, don't they? When they look at the night sky they see patterns of stars. I bet they dance, too!" Seeing Zane's anxious expression, he softened his tone. "Look, if Lenora can read alien messages while dreaming, there must be a way to write one they'll understand. She erased their message last night, so maybe she was planning to write one herself."

Zane shook his head. "No, she was protecting you."

"There must be a way!"

Zane's expression blanked out again. "There is," he said after a few seconds, "but you won't remember the details if I tell you now. Just use what you find in the dreamscape."

"Exploit the metaphor?"

"Exactly."

"So, can you can program it in time for tonight's run?"

Zane grinned. "No problem."

He jogged along the infinite beach, looking for the bottle. After what seemed like ages, he found it, half-buried in the sand. The blank sheet of paper lay nearby. He picked up his finds and resumed his search.

Next he spied a plank of rotting driftwood floating in the shallows. He prised a splinter free and dipped it in beach tar. His hands trembled as he held pen to paper.

But what should he write?

Despairing, he dropped his tools and walked to the water's edge. The urge to abandon his task washed over him, but he knew he could not. Instead, he scooped up handfuls of pebbles and rubbed them together, grinding out his frustration.

Finally inspiration came.

He dropped a pebble in the sand, then another, then several more, letting instinct guide his placements. When the pattern seemed right, he skipped from pebble to pebble, spinning three times at each marker. After a dozen repetitions he picked up the pebbles and started again.

He danced and danced until he fell to his knees, leaving just enough time to grab pen and paper before exhaustion tipped him into the void.

The perfect black sky glittered with stars.
Thousands of people arrived at the beach.
Each held a bottle plucked from the sea.
Each of them danced and then fell asleep.
And the aliens came…

The sun rose over the dunes.
The sun set over the sea.
Rose and set, rose and set.

But the dancers slept on.
So the aliens left.

Sand cupped his head as he stared at the azure sky. When he stretched out his arms, one hand landed on glass while the other slapped against paper.

He held the sheet at arm's length, shielding his eyes from the sun. The symbols meant nothing to him.

He rolled up the sheet and pushed it into the bottle. Now, how to seal it? He scoured the dune, found a screw top. Having secured the message, he waded into the water until waist-deep and threw the bottle far out to sea.

Relieved to have completed his task, he splashed in the shallows like a child until a yell jolted him from his play.

Looking along the beach, he saw her standing amid a group of men. One of them upended a bottle and tapped its base. A roll of paper fell into his hand. Before the man could read it he faded from view. The woman yelled at her remaining helpers, but they faded out too, one after another. She fell to her knees, weeping.

He knew he should flee, but the lure of her despair was too strong. As he drew near, she shuffled round to face him. Seeing her smile broke the spell.

He sprinted along the beach, pounding wet sand with his feet, but a glance over his shoulder revealed she was gaining. Though he dodged and weaved, her foot snagged his trailing leg and tumbled him into the sand. She loomed over him, thrusting a sheet of paper in his face.

Read this!

Thinking she would not risk soaking the paper, he crawled into the surf. Her hand snatched at his ankle, but he pulled free. Kicking hard, he dived into the breaking waves. He held his breath against straining lungs, willing himself to wake up.

A hand tugged at Jerome's shoulder, hastening his return to consciousness.

"Come on, get moving!" Zane sounded panicky.

"I'm going nowhere until I've seen Len—"

A piercing shriek cut him short.

"I'm taking her to hospital," said Zane. "She's even worse than her first time."

"You'll stay with her until she recovers?"

"Of course!"

"What about her disciples?"

"They're why you need to get moving!"

Jerome followed Zane out of his tent. Several men charged towards them, yelling obscenities. He sprinted for his truck. Bottles smashed against the hood as he floored the gas pedal.

It wasn't until he reached the Winthrop road that he remembered to switch on the radio. The NASA spokesman's voice boomed inside the cab.

"...We're now predicting the spacecraft will fly by at a distance of two million miles." A brief pause, then: "Sorry folks, they're just passing through."

Jerome pounded his fists against the steering wheel. This was not what he'd intended. Rather than tone down their messages, the aliens had evidently concluded that Humanity was not ready to dream with them. Thanks to Jerome, only Lenora had enjoyed that privilege.

No doubt she would regard him as her Judas.

That his actions had spared thousands of WhileAway users from mental injury did nothing to lift his mood. As he drove into the outskirts of Winthrop, his eyes filled with tears.

On the first anniversary of his encounter with Lenora, Jerome returned to Patterson Lake.

He had just finished lining up his 'scope on Mars when he felt a shove from behind. This time, despite stumbling, he managed to regain his balance. He tugged off his headphones and turned to face his assailant. Moonlight illuminated a familiar figure.

"Couldn't you just say 'hi'?"

Lenora flicked on her flashlight and pointed it at his face. Jerome peered through a fence of fingers, blinking away purple spots.

"Hurts your eyes, does it?" Her voice cut like broken glass. "Now imagine your brain overloaded in the same way!"

The thought made him shudder, but he didn't respond. Let her vent her fury; she had every right.

"I ran after you because I thought you could help, but you dived into the sea and disappeared." Her tone turned regretful. "I knew I didn't have long, so I read every message. There were dozens and dozens of them!"

Without warning, she threw herself at Jerome. He grabbed her wrists before her fists could hurt him.

"It was too much," she mumbled into his chest. "Dammit Jerome, I could have made it work if only you'd let me try!" He allowed her to pull back, but didn't let go.

"Lenora, you gave me no choice. If you had carried out your plan, the mental health of thousands of people would have been put at risk. I did the right thing!"

"If you believe sending the aliens away was the 'right thing', then yeah, job done!"

"That wasn't my intention," he said.

"Oh, I realise you didn't want that outcome, but that is what happened," said Lenora. "It was you who convinced the aliens that Humanity was too dumb to bother with." She snorted. "And I can see their point!"

Her frustration mirrored the feelings of billions of people worldwide. Fortunately for Jerome, Zane had done a thorough job of covering their tracks while also tending to Lenora.

"How long were you unconscious?"

"Six…frickin…months!"

He stared at her, open-mouthed.

"How do you feel now?"

"It's bearable during the day, but at night, when I'm dreaming, it's like I've got aliens living in my head." She tugged hard and broke free from his grip. "And I have you to thank for that."

Which was indubitably true and impossible to remedy.

"Have you learnt anything from your dreams? Like, where they come from?" He felt momentarily ashamed at letting his curiosity get the better of him, then told himself that the so-called experts hadn't found out even that much yet.

Lenora stepped over to the 'scope and swung it towards the zenith. "There," she said.

With the Moon so bright, Jerome couldn't make out Lenora's target even using averted vision, but he knew precisely where the 'scope was pointing.

He whistled long and low. "So far from home!"

She nodded. "Two million light years, give or take."

"What a story they'd have told us." Even as he spoke the words, he wished he could suck them out of the air. He held his hands out, begging forgiveness. To his surprise, her expression softened.

"Every night, a little of that story plays in here." She tapped her forehead. "But I can't make sense of it. For that, I need help."

"I'll do anything," he said.

Lenora took his hand and led him to her jeep, which she'd parked next to his truck while he stargazed to Holst. She opened the door and picked up two WhileAway consoles from the passenger seat.

"During my quieter phases, Zane coded up a new version of the software." Seeing Jerome's anxious expression, she added: "Don't worry, it runs off-line. Zane figured that when I'd recovered I might need a way to share my dreams."

Jerome chuckled. "Two heads being better than one?"

She nodded. "But Zane was too scared to try it."

In truth, the prospect terrified Jerome too; but it made sense to test Zane's farewell present before Lenora sought out new disciples, as she surely would.

"Let's get started then."

By the time Jerome crawled from his tent, the sun had risen over the hills. As he walked along the lakeside path, his mind's eye superimposed an image of blue-pelted, ape-like creatures cavorting on a beach of amber sand beneath a jet-black sky.

The aliens' never-ending dance must mean something, he told himself, but he had no idea what. They might have been electing a new leader, for all he knew. Sharing Lenora's dream had left him with a pounding headache but no particular insights.

Where was Lenora? Hiking in the hills, most likely. Doubtless working off some of that rage. When she returned, they could talk some more. He would try to explain, again, why he'd refused to sleep with her last night.

In the meantime, he had some new dance steps to try out.

STRING-DRIVEN THING

When it comes to generating energy, Robert Heinlein's maxim definitely applies: "There ain't no such thing as a free lunch." For now, the sun continues to shine. If it stops any time soon I guess you'll have a few hours, at most, to blame me.

Belinda and I first heard about extracting zero-point energy from the vacuum long before the news feeds got excited. Invariably the earliest of early adopters, we ordered a box of zero-point light bulbs as soon as we read the press release, despite the outrageous price. Set to hover, they made lovely Christmas ornaments.

Whoever said that perpetual motion doesn't work?

On the Twelfth day of Christmas Belinda switched off the lowermost bulb and let it fall into her hand.

"Oh!" she yelped.

Worried that she might have scorched her hand, I swivelled in my chair.

"Did you burn yourself?"

Belinda served up her minted you're-such-a-dummy look. "Oh, Mike; you're not going senile on me, are you?" At which point I recalled that zero-point devices operate at ambient temperature.

"What's up then?"

"Not sure yet."

She was peering intently at what, from my vantage point, looked like nothing at all. First she bent down; then she stood on tip-toe; finally she crabbed around, bobbing her head, inspecting whatever it was, or wasn't, from every angle. Finally she gave a little nod accompanied by a grunt of satisfaction.

"Okay, take a look at the rug. From here." She indicated a point in mid-air with the tip of her index finger.

We really should have got rid of that fraying memento of our honeymoon years ago, but I peered at it as instructed. A small patch looked decidedly pale. Had I spilt something on it? No, evidently not, because when I raised my head the faded patch moved too.

"Oh, my!"

"Indeed," said Belinda.

I experimented some more. By looking through the designated spot from various directions I could make patches of wallpaper and curtains fade.

Now it was my turn to point at the flaw in space. "Is that where you hung the light, darling?"

"No, that's where you hung it!"

I accepted the blame with a sigh before resuming my inspection of the defect. Something had caught my eye: a tiny nub of whiteness where previously there was nothing.

"Unless I'm much mistaken," I said, "there is something here now."

With my thumbnail and forefinger pinched together, I attempted to tweeze it out. On my third attempt, I finally managed to extract a short piece of what looked remarkably like string.

"Now you've done it," Belinda said.

How right she was.

That evening, I fired up my laptop and sent an e-mail to BBC News. My announcement retained "most read" status for a fortnight. I suppose someone had to be first to report the phenomenon, which is how the Jamison Effect came to be so-named.

Before long, everyone was pulling string out of nothing. A forgotten generation of cosmologists presumably jumped for joy, albeit arthritically.

A few learned voices did express concern, but most folk continued to run their vacuum energy bulbs and other zero-point devices without batting an eyelid. As for me, well, I reverted to cranking the power handle on my laptop. Scuffing up the Universe just didn't feel right, somehow.

Now, the thing about string is that it's such a versatile material, particularly useful in these resource-limited times. Belinda, bless her, decide to knit me a string vest, but I made her wear it, because, to be frank, seeing her dressed like that did something wicked to my libido.

"Tie a knot in it, darling," she said, favouring me with a lascivious wink. I'm pretty sure she wasn't referring to the string-based necktie she'd sewn up a couple of days before, the topology of which I was still attempting to tame.

Similar scenes of blissful domesticity doubtless typified the all-too-brief era of free energy. The associated glut of string led to a cornucopia of crafts-based competitions and concerts for music played exclusively on "stringed" instruments. Who other than me cared about the growing number of bare patches?

A killjoy physicist working for the Russian Academy of Sciences, that's who. Kudos to him, I say. He measured the speed of light every month for a year, achieving unprecedented accuracy. His paper in Nature caused a sensation. Further experiments revealed that the elementary charge had increased slightly. Evidently the universe's fundamental constants weren't so constant any more. True, the changes were tiny, but that wasn't the point.

The more pieces of cosmic string we pulled from thin air, the more deltas we inflicted on the fine structure constant. And as more than one eminent scientist has observed, the fundamental properties of our universe do seem exquisitely fine-tuned for the existence of life. How many hits can alpha take before that observation no longer holds true? No one knows for sure, but I know that I never used to get this nervous before sunrise.

Only the other day, the government announced personal quotas for harvesting zero-point energy, plus a string-trading scheme. But for me, such measures don't go nearly far enough.

So, Belinda and I have bitten the bullet and declared our house a string-free zone. From now on, we'll be relying on solar power. We're the first of the un-adopters and we'll trumpet our conversion to anyone who'll listen, because the world has to learn that energy is never free.

FIRST AND THIRD

The Martian twilight had deepened to the point where Joe Engels no longer trusted himself to keep his Norton Warmonger on the blacktop. Just a little further, he told himself. And sure enough, two kliks down the road, the bike's headlight beam picked out a billboard. As he eased the fat-tyred, nuclear-powered machine to a halt, he thanked the gods of corporate irrationality for installing a public portal in the middle of nowhere. Three years into her post-life, Masie still insisted on a view of the physical world, not merely his ugly face. Calling her from a hacked motel vidphone was a no-no, even at night.

After unpacking the Norton's panniers, Joe set his camping dome to inflate and then switched the bike's stealth field generator to wide-area mode. Can't be too careful, he told himself, even though the risk of being spied on by a satellite was minimal.

While gazing at the purpling sky, Joe noticed a speck of light moving so fast it couldn't be Deimos. Suddenly it flared like a nova: so bright and "Look at that!" and gone on the count of ten. Despite having retired from the 'jacking game, Joe continued to count seconds like they meant the difference between life and death.

Possibly one of Masie's fellow post-lifers had just made the grade, although why anyone wanted to pilot a robotic spacecraft on a mission lasting millennia baffled him. Masie herself stood no chance of graduating from Ad Astra, but that wasn't why he'd placed her there.

Joe shivered inside his Mars-suit. His conversation with Masie would be annoyingly brief, as the temperature would soon dip to minus fifty: downright balmy according to older colonists, but too cold for him to remain outside the dome for long.

Joe bounced-cum-waddled over to the billboard, taking care to avoid the omnipresent pits and boulders. As he drew near, a quartet of solar-powered floodlights illuminated him. Twin surveillance cameras mounted on the top of the unit twitched, converging their gaze on him. Masie flashed up on the screen, her Technicolor dreadlocks and ebony skin flawlessly rendered in 3D. Seeing her plump ruby lips caught mid-pout made Joe's heart flutter. Then he saw the ribbon of text running beneath her unmoving face and his mood turned to despair.

<< Masie says: Hello >>

Evidently Acme Afterlife Inc. had downgraded Masie to their cheapest policy again—their way of telling Joe to pay up or else. In truth, he'd not stopped paying up these past three years. Moving Masie to Acme's Ad Astra domain had been a worryingly expensive attempt to keep her safe from prying eyes.

"Hi honey," he said, trying not to sound anxious.

<< Masie asks: Why are you late? >>

So stilted, so polite, so not like Masie.

Joe sighed. "My bike broke down."

He'd wasted two hours fixing the out-of-whack gyros, which explained why he'd ended up camping one hundred kliks short of Valles Midway.

<< Masie says: That is what happens if you buy a second-hand motorcycle instead of stealing a new one. >>

"I'm doing my best, honey."

<< Masie says: Your best is not good enough. >>

"I've got a maintenance job booked for tomorrow." Masie didn't have to "say" what she thought of that; the triplet of exclamation marks sufficed. "The money's not so bad," he added.

<< Masie asks: Will it pay for her upgrade to First? >>

"Yes, honey." He didn't dare add that it would last a week at most.

<< Masie says: Then you should get on with it. >>

Seeing Masie's favourite phrase made Joe smile, but before he could respond the Acme logo erased her image. Joe waddled back to the dome, cursing under his breath. "Talking" to Masie in Third sucked worse than a hole in a pressure suit.

The pressure readout on the dome's external panel registered 75% of Earth normal, which was the best Joe could expect from this much-patched example of surveyor's equipment. Once through the airlock, he took off his helmet, wriggled his nose at the chemical tang produced by the CO_2 scrubbers and began unpacking his belongings.

Later, he sat on his bedroll slurping lukewarm tomato soup and occasionally remembering to wipe his beard. Since Masie's death there had been no one to scold him about his sloppy manners, no one to share life on the road. Born within a day's horse-ride of the Grand Canyon, Masie would have loved Valles Marineris. Speeding along the highway that afternoon, the terraced features of the colossal rift valley had reminded him of folded blankets—and bedtime with Masie.

Tears pricked his eyes.

"Get on with it," he whispered.

The wide-eyed look Joe received from his client's departing customer made him feel uneasy, but on entering the boudoir he saw nothing unusual. The transparent waterbed and pink fur carpet were standard issue, likewise the cleansing cubicle and walk-in closet—which presumably housed the usual outfits and appliances. Then he spotted the boudoir's occupant and instantly revised his opinion. There was no mistaking that combo of sculpted crimson hairdo, voluptuous physique and doll-like face. He hadn't seen a Lyra in years; indeed, had hoped never to do so again. Given the circumstances of Masie's death, who could blame him?

None of which made it any less strange that this example had avoided the remodelling shop. After all, the vogue for replicating mid-21st Century pop stars, which had briefly swamped the market with facsimiles of Lyra Belini and her peers, was long past. Joe glanced at the bot's naked backside and gave an involuntary shudder.

Oh, just get on with it, he said to himself.

According to the pimp who had phoned in the service request, a terrified customer had reported a seizure. Joe selected a scanner from his toolkit and ran the usual diagnostics. The Lyra's neural parameters showed green across the board. He shrugged and rebooted the bot. Easy money!

When the Lyra reawakened, he held out his pad. "That'll be five hundred credits."

The scarcity of bot engineers on Mars accounted for the outrageous price—that and Acme's payment plan.

The Lyra pouted so provocatively she made Masie look innocent. "How about payment in kind?"

Uh-oh, Joe said under his breath. No way would he trade credits for quickies. Doing it with a probot would be a no-no even if Masie didn't need the money. In any case, he wasn't about to let the pimp renege on the deal.

Joe snatched a neural baseliner from his toolbox and held the tip of the pen-shaped device under the Lyra's nose. "Five hundred credits right now, or I shove this up your left nostril." The neubaser no longer worked, but the bot didn't know that.

The Lyra gaped at Joe, apparently startled into silence by his threat. Then a nasal voice brayed forth—the pimp on override.

"Guess you must really need the money, what with you waving that highly illegal piece of kit around." Joe lowered the neubaser. The pimp continued: "That's better. Shall we say fifty?"

Joe folded his arms and gave the bot his sternest look, hoping that bravado might carry the day. "Payment in full or I report this establishment."

The Lyra tilted its head to one side. "Oh, I reckon the authorities would be a whole lot more interested in any report I might file on you. Done any 'jacking, bud?"

Joe heard a snigger. The Martian police were reliably ineffectual, but the pimp evidently recognised that Joe dared not take the risk. A thirty-stretch in Ceres Gaol would put an end to his money problems once and for all— and put an end to Masie, too.

"Okay," he sighed. "Fifty it is."

"And there I was thinking we'd settled on twenty-five."

Joe acquiesced before the price could fall further.

The Lyra winked at him. "You're my kind of guy."

Cursing his luck, Joe snatched up his toolkit and waddled into the corridor, where he bumped into the Lyra's next customer.

"Good luck in there," he snarled.

Standing outside the brothel under the milky blue sky, Joe contemplated Midway's main drag, with its motley collection of Mars-suited miners and dust-streaked robo-trucks. For all Nu-Mars Inc's boasts of self-maintaining highways and a thickening atmosphere, Mankind's Second Home looked jaded already.

Cursing his luck, Joe settled onto the Norton, gunned the engine and rode out of town, vowing never to return.

As Joe neared the first billboard beyond Midway, he steered the Norton off the road, throwing rooster tails of dust into the skinny air and provoking a fusillade of flashes from a passing ore-truck. As if on cue, Masie appeared. Despite her scowling expression, Joe risked a smile. He might not be forgiven but at least Masie was back in First.

"How's my favourite space cadet?"

A growl came over his headphones. "Oh, just dandy!"

"What's up honey?"

Masie rolled her eyes. "Post-life is fricking hard work, Joe, in case you hadn't noticed."

"Honey—"

"And it's harder still when I'm stuck in Third!"

He held out his gloved hands in a gesture of apology. "I'm transferring every credit I make into your account, but bot maintenance don't pay so good." Particularly in the less respectable sectors of the Martian economy.

Masie scowled at him. "Bot maintenance? Next you'll be trying out for a desk job! We used to make money from 'jacking. What's stopping you now?"

What had happened to Masie in Tucson was Joe's reason, but he knew better than to remind her.

"Honey," he groaned, "I can't turn back the clock."

If only, he said to himself.

The five years they'd spent roaming the sun-baked towns of the American West, 'jacking bots and putting them to work stealing titanium, copper and selenium, had been the happiest of his life. Dubbed "The New Bonnie and Clyde" by the more sensationalist news-feeds, they had worked hard to live up to their forerunners' reputation. Now, Joe found himself working no less hard, if considerably less violently, to ensure Masie's continuing presence on Ad Astra.

She nodded, as if she'd read his mind. "Time of our lives, wasn't it?"

"Yeah, I sure miss it."

Suddenly Masie's eyes blazed. "Not half as much as you'll miss me if my account hits zero!"

Joe sighed. "I'm doing everything I can."

As usual, Masie had some ideas on that score.

"Why don't you sell your neubaser? It's no use if you're not 'jacking bots! And what about that set of q-chips you keep in your toolbox?"

Joe dismissed her advice with a shake of his head. No way would he'd ever sell his tools! Exasperated by her attitude, he turned away and gazed at the sky.

Masie's laughter rang in his ears. "Well I'm sure as shit not heading up there, sweetheart. Heaven knows why you chose starship pilot school for me. We both know I ain't ever gonna make Rapture."

Which was surely true, thought Joe, but that wasn't why he'd placed Masie there.

"Honey, I chose Ad Astra because it's the last place the authorities would think to look for you. You know that!"

But Masie wasn't listening.

"...Plus this is the most boring post-life yet! It's like being back at college, with lectures and lab classes and all, but without the sex, drugs and all-night parties." She rolled her eyes. "There's not even any shopping!"

Joe shook his head in dismay. Ad Astra might lack opportunities for retail therapy, but Acme's industry-leading privacy policy more than made up for it.

"Honey, you're missing the point!"

"...And then imagine not being able to gossip with your fellow post-lifers 'cos some tightwad hasn't paid the fricking bill!"

"Honey, that's not fair!"

"Life ain't fair, sweetheart. Post-life even less so."

He let her rant on, knowing that if their positions were reversed he'd need an outlet too. The sigh that ended her tirade made him shiver.

"Sweetheart," she said, her voice suddenly husky, "I miss you so bad."

"I miss you too, honey." He wanted so desperately to hug her. "I wish I could make post-life better for you..."

"Oh, don't fret," she scolded. "Ad Astra ain't so bad. We do have some fun, but this is not what you'd call a comfortable post-life. Lately, we've had some disappearances..."

A series of increasingly loud beeps came over Joe's headphones. "Honey," he said, "I think you'd better—"

"Take Johnny Gleason, for example. Well, something did! I heard he was flush with money, but—"

Masie's face froze with her mouth wide-open. On the count of five, a line of text began crawling beneath her static image.

<< Masie says: Please send more money. >>

"Yes, honey."

Feeling too numb to say anything more, Joe climbed onto his Norton. Somehow, he'd make enough money to get Masie reinstated in First. Rapture might be hopelessly out of reach, but he'd do right by her. And if the credits ever did run out, he'd not outlive her by more than a few seconds. Opening his helmet to the Martian sky might not seem worthy of The New Bonnie and Clyde, but he'd do it all the same.

In life as in death, there was no escaping Masie.

A hundred kliks east of Midway, Joe hustled the Norton through one of Valles Highway's sweeping bends while singing along to Born to be Wild. He loved the raw power of Twentieth Century rock, however archaic it sounded to everybody else, including Masie.

He had just argued himself out of resuming his 'jacking career when an incoming call silenced the music. His head-up display presented the ID of the Lyra from Midway. He dismissed the call with a snarled expletive. Two bends later, the trilling resumed. Despite his misgivings, he took the call.

"Mr Engels, I need your help."

The probot's voice sounded odd, not at all like a Lyra. Why had its slime-ball of a pimp re-voiced it now? Joe frowned as he eased off the throttle.

"I repair obsolete bots on a 'reasonable efforts' basis," he said, trying to keep his tone business-like. "If you read the contract's small print, you'll find there's no guarantee." As the Norton rolled to a halt he realised that something besides the bot's anomalous voice was making his brain itch.

"Why aren't I talking to your pimp?"

The bot ignored his question. "Please," it begged. "You must get me out of here!"

This unexpected plea flummoxed Joe. Rescuing a probot would surely prove futile, for where else could it work except in a brothel? Still, its display of emotion had piqued his curiosity. According to Masie, bots didn't feel much of anything.

"Get you out of where exactly?"

The Lyra didn't answer immediately. Instead Joe heard two new voices over the link, neither of which sounded like the bot nor, indeed, its pimp.

He tongued the volume control higher, but still couldn't make out what was being said. Sensing a possible threat, he decided to press on rather than concern himself with this bot's problem.

"Look, I'm on a call, so—"

"I can make it worth your while," said the bot. "Is five thousand credits enough?"

Joe gasped. Where had the bot got that kind of money? If from the pimp, well, that begged a mighty big question. Still, he'd gladly run back to Midway for such a sizeable payday. Assuming, of course, this wasn't another con.

"Half up front," he replied.

"Ha! Why should I trust you not to ride off with the money?"

Despite the bot nixing his spur-of-the-moment plan, he still needed something up front for Masie's sake, just in case he couldn't complete the job. A week's worth of First would do.

"Five hundred or you find someone else."

He counted to twenty before the bot replied with a reluctant sounding "Okay". Presumably it had tried but failed to find an alternative supplier of maintenance services.

"Then we have a deal," he said, sounding calmer than he felt. In this business, an advance was rarer than a Martian barbeque. "As soon as I receive confirmation of your payment, I'll head straight back."

Excepting a stop-off to tell Masie the good news.

Joe had expected to see Masie smile when he walked up to the billboard, whereas the way her eyes darted reminded him of a mouse looking out for a cat. Instinct made him look over his shoulder. He saw dust settling on the blacktop, nothing more.

"What's up honey?"

"We've got a Reaper in Ad Astra!" Masie sounded as worried as she looked. Joe held up his gloved hands in a calming gesture.

"Honey, your money worries are over! I've just been paid an advance, which is why you're back in First. And when I complete this job you'll be safe from downgrading for months, never mind deletion."

Masie gave Joe a look that reminded him of every 'jacking that had gone wrong. There had been a few.

"I don't mean deletion," she snapped. "I've seen what happens when the money runs out. Blink and you'd miss it!" She paused as if recalling the demise of a fellow post-lifer. "No, I hear this thing is real grad-u-al, like it's wiping your mind one terabyte at a time."

Masie's description made no sense to Joe. What else could this Reaper be except Ad Astra's deletion process? The cops that had hounded Masie out of her previous domains were tangible presences, as required by post-life law.

"Have you actually seen this Reaper?"

Masie rolled her eyes. "Of course not! 'Cos if I had, I'd be dead and you'd be talking to the Acme logo!"

"Are you're sure this isn't just Acme trying to keep you post-lifers honest? 'Make Rapture or you meet the Reaper', that kind of thing."

Masie shook her head. "Why would they bother? Most of us are going nowhere, we know that." And Joe knew better than to argue the point. Masie continued: "Anyway, this isn't the first time. There was a story doing the rounds just before you moved me on from Mall of Light. I didn't tell you because I figured it for a post-life myth. But after I emerged from Third this morning, I did some digging. Turns out this Reaper appeared in Gates of Paradise too, just before I got kicked out of there."

"And you think it might have done for Gleason?"

"Worse than that, it's just wiped Sarah Klein!"

"Who's she?"

"Klein's next in line for Rapture. Or rather she was until she got sucked into oblivion by this thing!"

"Okay, but that doesn't mean—"

Masie eyes glittered with panic. "Gleason's not in my class, but Klein is! So now do you understand why I'm scared? Each time the Reaper strikes, it's one step closer to me!"

Joe felt halfway to terror himself. "What can I do?"

"Unless you know of another domain to hide me in, not a fricking thing."

Masie sounded defeated and with good reason. If Acme couldn't keep her safe, no other post-life service provider could. Joe smacked his hand into his fist.

"There must be something!"

Masie shook her head. "Just keep paying up, until either I make Rapture or..." Her gloomy expression made it clear which outcome she expected.

"Masie, honey, I—" He bit down on the platitude. Judging by Masie's jittery expression, something had just spooked her.

"Gotta fly," she said.

The Acme logo erased her face. A corporate slogan taunted Joe with promises of the digital hereafter. Though tempted, he resisted the urge to throw rocks at the billboard. He might still need its facilities, assuming the Reaper hadn't found Masie.

Dismayed by his inability to help his beloved, Joe rode on into Midway.

The door to the Lyra's boudoir stood slightly ajar. Joe pushed it open but hesitated on the threshold. He half-expected to see the pimp's body, at least some telltale spots of blood amid the fur. The prospect of dealing with a rogue bot made him twitchy. He was on the point of backing out when the Lyra emerged from the closet. At least this time it was wearing clothes: the ubiquitous French maid's outfit.

"Please," it begged, "you've got to get me out of here!"

Bemused by this request, Joe asked, "Where's your pimp?"

Without warning, the bot grabbed his right arm. Joe knew better than to resist. For all its sex-kitten appearance, a Lyra easily surpassed him for strength.

"Oh, I scared him right out of town," it replied.

The blood drained from his face. Never before had he felt scared of a bot, not even in Tucson. To his surprise, this one let go of his arm. Briefly, he considered following the pimp's example and hightailing it out of Midway, but he knew what Masie would say to such financial dereliction. Instead, he took a deep breath to calm his nerves.

"Okay," he said, "so now you're a free agent. But unless you've got a diagnosable fault, I don't see how I can help."

The bot rolled its eyes. "Free agent? What a laugh!"

"How do you mean?"

The probot fell backwards onto the waterbed, which quivered glutinously in the low gravity. To his surprise, it flashed a typical Lyra smile, all gleaming teeth and baby blues, like he was just another customer.

"Wanna make waves with me, mister?"

Joe whistled relief. The Lyra's come-on might be laughably unsubtle but it did represent normal behaviour. And the voice sounded right, too. But what, he wondered, had caused this personality flip-flop?

"Let's stick to business, shall we?"

"Oh, you're such a tease!"

Ignoring the mockery, Joe said, "Okay, here's what we'll do. I'll run a deep scan. If I find out what's wrong and fix it, you pay me in full. There'll be no payment in kind, or making waves, or any other such nonsense. Got that?"

He received a compliant nod from the Lyra.

"Right then," said Joe. "Let's flip your lid."

The Lyra obligingly tipped its head forward. Joe peeled away its crimson wig and pressed the stud on the back of its neck. Then he paused. Despite ten years of experience operating on bots, opening the skull still made him uneasy. His imagination conjured up a quivering lump of grey matter, just like in Masie's favourite old movies, not the cluster of q-chips nestling within a web of sensor feeds that he actually found. Yet this familiar sight didn't make him feel any less anxious, because the prospect of performing a deep scan on a Lyra evoked all-too vivid memories of Tucson.

They had spent hours staking out a strip-joint before finally snaring the Lyra. Masie had just hooked up her cortical implant to its brain when her body jerked like she'd grabbed a live cable. Before Joe could react, she slumped to the ground unconscious. Fighting the urge to panic, he ran a deep scan and discovered that one of the bot's q-chips had dumped a virus into Masie's implant. Unable to pull her out of the mind-link without leaving her brain-dead, he bundled bot and beloved into his van and drove off.

That evening, with police sirens Dopplering closer and Masie still inextricably bot-linked, he had bootstrapped her upload from backup to the cheapest PLSP. As soon as the transfer completed, he drove off into the Arizona night, leaving Masie and her nemesis to their fate.

The next ten months were the worst of his life. It wasn't until he disembarked in Port Lowell that he glimpsed Masie again, scowling at him from a billboard.

Joe shook his head. Get on with it, he told himself.

After hooking up the last of the neural probes, Joe commenced the scan.

"Anything?" the bot asked in its non-Lyra voice.

Joe leaned back and stared at the bot. Possibly the deep scan had toggled between two competing personalities: the default Lyra and a God-knows-what. He double-checked the diagnostics, but found nothing suspicious.

"Looks like I'll have to dig a bit deeper."

Which meant he'd have to establish a direct mind-link, thus replicating the very procedure that had fried Masie's mind.

"You melt me when you're messing with my mind," the bot chanted.

"Oh, very funny," said Joe, recognising a line from Lyra Belini's most famous song. "Now be quiet!"

Lacking Masie's finesse, it took him almost an hour to configure the link. After muttering a prayer, he activated his own cortical implant for the first time since Masie's death. To his astonishment, images from Tucson flashed into his mind. Downright weird images too, considering that at no stage had he lain down on the parking lot, let alone looked up at a younger, moustachioed version of himself, who seemed to be leaning over him; no, over Masie; no, over him...

Then the truth dawned. Those were not his memories!

Trembling with fear, Joe pulled free of the link. "Got to go," he mumbled, backing away. He wanted nothing more to do with this deranged bot.

"Fifty thousand credits!" it shrieked.

Joe gaped at the bot, stunned by its extraordinary offer. How could he possibly turn down a payment that would keep Masie in First for years? Yet the urge to flee remained strong. He was still dithering when the bot grabbed both of his arms and shook them hard.

"Please, you've got to —"

"Get me out of here," Joe parroted. But how could anyone get the "me" out of a bot, when its brainpan contained nothing but q-chips and programming? He shook his head. "Sorry, I don't understand!"

"You used to 'jack bots, right?"

Joe played for time. "What of it?"

"Well, this bot has gone and 'jacked me!"

Which begged another mighty big question. This time he dared to ask it. "So, who are you?"

"I'm Sarah Klein."

Joe gaped at the bot. Then he shook his head, dumbfounded by its declaration. Believing that a Reaper had wiped Klein from Ad Astra was one thing, accepting that this bot now hosted her mental essence quite another. Sure, uploading a deceased person from backup had long ago become commonplace, but that was child's play compared with downloading a post-lifer into a bot. Joe had never heard of such a thing.

"That's impossible," he said. But observing the bot's tight-lipped expression made him immediately doubt his assertion. After all, why should it falsely claim to be Klein? That, too, seemed impossible. But he knew a way to test the claim.

"If you're really Sarah Klein, then you've met Masie Obermeyer. And sure as Acme makes money she'll have told you how we met." Masie could be relied to keep most secrets, but not that one.

The bot giggled. "Not many men can claim to have been rescued by their future partner from a Kansas City brothel."

He gave Klein a sour look. "Okay, I guess you're for real. But I don't understand what you want me to do!"

"I know you uploaded Masie illegally, so I'm offering to reward you handsomely if you'll do the same for me." She held out a hand. "Do we have a deal?"

Joe rubbed his chin while he pondered her request. Perhaps he could undo the Reaper's handiwork and earn a small fortune in the process, but why bother? Couldn't he just wait for the Reaper to download Masie? Sooner or later, it would catch up with Masie. Which would be bad luck on Klein, of course.

Joe glanced at the probot and winced. Masie would hate her new home, but given a choice between a futile, not to mention ruinously expensive, pursuit of Rapture and a return, however compromised, to the physical world, he knew which way she'd jump. To regain his beloved, all he had to do was wait. The five hundred credits Klein had already paid him ought to keep Masie in First long enough for the Reaper to harvest her.

He shook his head. "No, I don't think so."

Klein's gaze narrowed. "I thought you needed the money."

"Not anymore."

Klein scowled at him, as if only now realising her mistake. Then her frown turned to a smile so smug it nearly stopped Joe's heart. What had he forgotten?

"In that case Mr Engels, there are two things you should know. Firstly—" She opened the bot's mouth wide. Joe heard an official-sounding voice. This time he could make out the man's words.

"Tracking...Valles region...ETA Midway..."

Klein tilted her head to one side. "Guess who recovered this bot after you abandoned it in Tucson."

Evidently the cops were onto him, though not yet sure of his location. But if they could pinpoint him, they'd surely have no qualms about using a little pre-emptive EMP, which would fry his bike's stealth field generator not to mention the probot. So waiting for Masie to download wasn't an option after all.

"Can you scramble the tracker?"

Klein grinned. "If you guarantee to upload me onto Ad Astra, I promise to wipe the entanglement."

"Okay... And the second thing I should know is?"

"What makes you think Masie will survive downloading?"

"You managed it."

"Ah, but I've reviewed this probot's memories prior to my arrival. There is a history of erratic behaviour, but no signs that Johnny Gleason and co ever attained consciousness. Seems like I was the first to stick. Frankly, that doesn't surprise me at all."

No wonder Klein had come top of her class, mused Joe. Someone who could cope with being downloaded into a malfunctioning bot would doubtless savour the task of captaining the slow boat to Alpha Centauri. That Klein so desperately wanted to pursue her destiny in deep space rather than remain a fortuitous physical presence on Mars told Joe a lot. She seemed less human than most bots. Which begged the most important question of all.

"If I promise to re-upload you, will you ensure that Masie downloads safely?"

"I can try."

"Trying ain't good enough!"

Klein shrugged. "Masie and I will both be taking a huge risk. But yes, I think I can make it work for her."

After briefly considering the alternative, Joe held out his hand. Klein shook it carefully.

But negotiating this bargain of necessity was the easy part, Joe reflected.

Assuming he could subvert the Acme link, he'd have figure how to accomplish a synchronised two-way personality transfer. That, he felt sure, had never been attempted before.

All this with the cops closing in!

"Tell me Ms Klein," he said, "have you ever ridden pillion?"

Klein grimaced. "This bot has done a lot of things I never have and would never want to," she said, smiling primly. "But I don't believe it has ever ridden a motorbike."

Not a bit like Masie, Joe said to himself, as he followed Klein out of the brothel.

Masie had just begun recounting how she'd avoided the Reaper when the billboard cameras panned away from Joe. Her eyes blazed from the screen like twin death rays.

"Can't say I blame you for dipping your wick given where I am and all, but turning up with a probot in tow—that's just rubbing my face in it!" The cameras zoomed in on Klein. "And damn me if it ain't a fricking Lyra!"

Klein performed a curtsy. "Not just any old Lyra, my dear. I believe you have history with this one."

Masie wrinkled her nose as if she'd just stepped on a dog turd. "Joe, tell me that ain't the Tucson bot!"

He held up his gloved palms. "Afraid so."

Masie's image blanked out.

Klein grunted contemptuously. "Now what?"

"We cut her some slack."

Masie reappeared on the count of twenty, as Joe guessed she would, though he hadn't expected her to look so shamefaced.

"First of all, I know you've never cheated on me. I shouldn't have implied that you had. Wouldn't have been cheating anyway."

Joe shrugged but said nothing.

"Secondly, you've never wasted my time. So you must have brought this thing here for a reason." She shot his companion a vicious stare before turning back to him. "Which would be?"

Klein butted in before Joe could answer.

"Don't you recognise my voice?"

"Sure I do, though why anyone would re-voice a probot so it sounded like..." She paused, as if suddenly unsure of her reasoning. Then her eyes bugged. "No way!" she exclaimed. "Just no fricking way!"

Klein groaned. "Why would I deceive you?"

Joe made a quelling gesture. A feud was the last thing he needed. He turned to Masie. Now it was his turn to look shamefaced, as he began his long-delayed explanation.

"After I got us back to the motel, I was in such a hurry to begin the upload I didn't have time to un-hook you from the Lyra." Which wasn't precisely true, but this didn't seem the moment to admit that he'd lacked the skill to disentangle Masie without leaving her brain-dead. Needless to say, the judiciary had shown no such qualms.

Masie rolled her eyes. "I might have known!"

Joe continued. "When I scanned you, I discovered that your brain had gone into spasm because one of the Lyra's q-chips had planted a proof-of-concept virus in your implant. So when I uploaded you via your implant the virus hitched a ride to the PLSP server. There it deployed the Reaper, which has been downloading post-lifers into this bot ever since, copying itself from one domain to another while searching for you. Doubtless each owner saw the bot throw a fit, tried to fix it and then traded it on." He turned to Klein who confirmed his intuition with a nod.

"When the cops learned of my emigration they tagged the bot and shipped it to Mars, reasoning that it would eventually find its way to this planet's premier bot fixer. So now it's here, still waiting for the Reaper to reunite its body and your soul."

"Trust me," Klein sneered. "You're a perfect match."

Masie ignored the barb. "Sweetheart, if you seriously think I'm gonna spend the rest of my life in that thing..."

Joe made a beseeching gesture. "Honey, there's no avoiding the Reaper. Sooner or later it will download you."

The billboard cameras twitched as Masie turned to Klein. She grinned wolfishly.

"So, why don't I just wait?"

Joe turned to Klein and mouthed, "Make it brief." Klein nodded. "My dear, it's like this..." When she finished, he added: "So, we need her help to ensure you download compos mentis—and she needs our help to get back to where she belongs."

Masie puffed out her cheeks and then slowly expelled her virtual breath, a sign that he'd won her over.

"Okay," she said, still frowning. "So how exactly are you going to make this work?"

Joe smiled at her, hoping to instil confidence that he scarcely felt. "I'll open a covert channel to Ad Astra and configure it for duplex operation. As soon as the Reaper starts downloading you, it will trigger a simultaneous upload from my spare q-chip set, which will contain a copy of Klein. As the transfer proceeds, she will gradually fade out of the bot at the same rate your own presence builds up." Klein would also have to suppress the bot's Lyra personality, so it didn't get in Masie's way. He turned to her and received a nod of approval. "So, with a little luck—"

"With a little luck?" Masie shook her head in dismay. "I need a fricking miracle!"

Klein chuckled. "You and me both, my dear. But since this is the only game in town, I suggest we get on with it!"

Before the cops find us, Joe muttered beneath his breath while crossing his fingers, no easy task while wearing Mars-gloves. Masie gave a reluctant nod.

Sighing with relief, Joe turned to Klein and made a lifting gesture with his fingers.

"Ready when you are, Ms Klein."

By the time Joe had configured the link to his satisfaction his shadow stretched halfway to the canyon walls. He imagined credits draining from Masie's account like sand in an egg timer. Entangling the neural states contained in the probot's q-chips with his own set had taken much longer than expected. But now, finally, he held a copy of Klein.

When he called Masie, she looked harried, as if she'd spent the entire time evading the Reaper.

"Are you ready yet?"

"I believe so." He turned to Klein, who nodded.

"Masie should experience a soft landing."

"Then let's..."

"...Get on with it!" the women chorused.

Joe tapped an icon on his pad, opening the channel.

Moments later, Masie jerked like someone had poked a gun in her back.

"It's here!" she shrieked. "The Reaper's found me!"

Joe glanced at his pad to confirm that Klein's download had begun. "Try to stay calm, honey,"

"Get me out of here, dammit!"

This involuntary echo of Klein made Joe shiver. He glanced at the bot. With its eyes closed, it looked asleep. Turning back to Masie, he said, "Let it take you, honey."

"I love—" Masie's voice cut out. A moment later, her face exploded.

Joe watched open-mouthed as multi-coloured fractals branched and spiralled, filling the billboard with dizzyingly complex patterns. The effect was enthralling, hypnotic, spellbinding...

Joe snapped out of his trance just as the visual chaos coalesced into the Acme logo. On checking his pad he saw that thirty minutes had elapsed. Before he could examine the transfer log an unfamiliar female face flashed up on the billboard. Her electric blue hair, ice-white complexion and coal-black eyes made a striking impression.

"Are you...?"

The woman nodded. "Yes, I'm Sarah Klein."

Joe punched the air. Sarah frowned at him like he was a misbehaving child.

"I've got to go," she said. "Thanks for everything."

"Wait a moment, what about—"

Klein's image vanished.

Which just left Masie, or so Joe fervently hoped. He struggled to remain calm while he deep-scanned the bot, which stood before him silent and unmoving. The diagnostics showed green, but they had all along. He commenced the reboot. He watched closely while the machine twitched into life. Eventually he could stand the suspense no longer.

"Masie?"

The probot's chin tipped up a fraction. A moist-looking tongue insinuated itself between crimson lips. Eyelids flickered then lifted . For a heart-thumping moment Joe dared to hope, but the look he received was pure probot: a Lyra's pouting come-on. Feeling sick at heart, he turned away. Masie's download had failed.

He was fiddling with his helmet's release latch when a neutral-sounding voice came over his headphones.

"Masie says: Hello."

Joe stared at the bot in disbelief. Trust Masie to make a joke out of her resurrection! Trembling with relief, he reached out to embrace her. Never mind that she didn't look or feel like the real thing, he'd got his beloved back.

"Welcome to the land of the living, honey!"

"Masie says: She is not sure this is living."

He grinned. "Okay honey, you can quit fooling now."

The shake of the head was slow as clockwork.

"Masie says: She is not fooling."

Joe fell to his knees and wept.

Oblivious to the chill seeping into his bones, Joe sat on a boulder facing the billboard. Sarah Klein had just finished greeting her fellow post-lifers on the Ad Astra campus lawn. A tumultuous cheer erupted as she rose, oh-so-gently, into the virtual sky. Soon, Klein would be piloting a starship carrying the seed of Humanity to new worlds unreachable by mere humans. Good luck to her, thought Joe.

A robotic hand squeezed his hip. Joe flinched.

"Masie says: You did your best."

Joe gave a mournful sigh. His best hadn't been good enough. Dazzled by the Reaper's visual pyrotechnics, he had failed to notice Acme downgrade Masie to Third as the transfer pushed her account below the critical threshold.

Better to have left his beloved in purgatory, he mused, than bring her back in this debased form.

A robotic arm cuddled his shoulders.

"Masie says: It is better than being dead."

He glanced at her and sighed. Maybe a skin-job would help.

"Masie says: Black might work."

Hearing a snatch of typical Masie humour lifted his spirits, but when he looked into her eyes, searching for further signs, she broke away. Something had caught her attention.

She pointed over his shoulder. "Masie says: Look at that!"

Turning as directed, he glimpsed a brilliant dot moving across the twilight sky. Must be Klein, he reasoned; outward bound for Alpha Centauri or wherever.

He glanced at Masie. "You okay about Klein?"

A grunt came over his headphones. "Klein's a bitch, but she does have the right stuff."

Joe stared at Masie, his mouth opening and closing without making a sound, while laughter filled his helmet. He smacked his gloved fist into palm.

"You lying, deceiving, daughter-of-a..."

Masie held out her arms. Joe stepped forward, expecting a hug. Instead he received a two-handed slap round the helmet that made his ears ring.

"That's for all the fricking downgrades, you useless foul-up of a partner!"

"Brought you back though, didn't I?"

Masie nodded, a little reluctantly maybe, but he needed no other forgiveness. They embraced tenderly. When he finally let go, she walked over to his Norton.

"So sweetheart, is there room for two on this clapped-out machine of yours?"

Joe grinned. "Yes, but you'll have to earn your keep!"

Masie gave him a look that would have slain a lesser man. "It's bad enough being hosted by a probot, but if you think I'm going on the Game, think again!"

Joe gave a rueful chuckle. "I swear I never thought of pimping you around Mars."

"Which leaves 'jacking!" Masie's voice crackled with excitement. "It'll be like old times."

Joe shook his head. "Not exactly, honey." Watching Klein's ascent had given him an idea.

"What do you mean?" Masie sounded unimpressed.

"I reckon we can use bots to salvage something much more valuable than metal." He grasped his partner's hands. "How many post-lifers make

Rapture?"

"Fewer than one in a thousand. Why?"

"Well, as far as I know, the Reaper is still present on Ad Astra, though hopefully dormant after completing its quest." He took a deep breath before continuing. "If we can reprogram it to download post-lifers into other bots we'll make ourselves a fortune! Of course, we'll need help from the virus's creator, who's probably still on Earth, or maybe not. But anyway, Klein reckoned your host's memories are fully accessible, so if you dig deep enough you should find some info on—"

Masie shrieked, "Stop yammering!"

Joe kept quiet while Masie did the math. On the count of twelve, she gave him a look that suggested he'd have to break the habit of a lifetime and sleep with a probot.

"Oh, you clever, clever man," she said, clapping her hands. "We can call ourselves The Resurrection Gang!"

In his mind's eye, Joe saw police drones flitting over a desert landscape, pursuing him and Masie from one 'jacking to the next, but never quite catching up.

Masie's warning growl interrupted his fantasy.

"Sweetheart, did Klein disable the tracker?"

Glancing along the road back to Midway, Joe saw lights moving in the distance. Might be miners, might be cops; it was hard to tell. Either way, it was time for the Resurrection Gang to burn rubber.

Joe fired up the Norton. Masie clambered onto the pillion and hugged him tight. With her love to make him bold, Joe felt like he could take on the world: Mars, Earth or wherever, it didn't matter to him.

"Get on with it!" Masie yelled.

Soundtracked by Joe's favourite rock song, they rode off into the night.

THE EYE PATCH PROTOCOL

Flying Officer Alan Woodruff went blind in one eye before the Vulcan left British airspace.

Less than thirty seconds of the four-minute warning remained when the quartet of Olympus engines thrust the gleaming, delta-winged behemoth into the air. As the bomber climbed steeply, heading for a rendezvous with a tanker over Norway, Woodruff reached out to pull the anti-flash blinds across the forward cockpit window.

He was maybe a second too late.

Woodruff blinked away tears but saw only blobs. Even so, he felt strangely calm as he moved the patch from his left eye to cover his right, which stung like hell. Compared to the destruction of the Port of Dover, however, his injury meant nothing.

Flight Lieutenant Freddie Jameson's clipped voice came over the intercom. "Just lost contact with Manston."

From the Air Electronics Officer's announcement Woodruff surmised that a second warhead had vaporised the RAF airbase that had been their temporary home since the dispersal order came into force. He tried to recall the faces of the ground crew who had worked so frantically to get the bomber airborne despite its dicky number three engine. At least they had died instantly. Countless civilians would not be so lucky.

Damn Khrushchev, damn Kennedy, and damn Castro too.

Woodruff looked to his left and saw Squadron Leader Leslie Harrington pull hard on the stick. The Vulcan seemed to stand on its tail as it climbed towards cruising altitude. Harrington, too, had discarded his eye patch.

"Reckon we can still fly this kite?"

Woodruff double-checked the cockpit windows before answering. Flying blind was one thing, flying with two blind pilots quite another.

"Roger that," he said.

The intercom crackled again. This time their AEO sounded ghoulishly chipper.

"Day-trip to Moscow, anyone?"

Ten minutes flying time from Moscow, Freddie Jameson confirmed

Woodruff's suspicion that the Vulcan would struggle to complete its bombing run.

"Incoming, vector one-sixty, climbing past fifty thousand, locked on."

Forced to operate with reduced thrust, the bomber could not out-climb its pursuer. Worse, with its electronic countermeasures system on the blink after one too many EM pulses, Freddie Jameson could not jam the MiG's radar.

"Autopilot off," announced Harrington, pulling hard on the stick. The Vulcan climbed sluggishly while banking to the east. Woodruff counted to thirty before Harrington spoke again.

"He's low on fuel."

Harrington meant the MiG, but Woodruff glanced at the bank of fuel gauges anyway. As co-pilot, his main task was to move fuel between the Vulcan's tanks while keeping the aircraft trimmed. The aerobatics he left to his captain.

Woodruff heard Flight Sergeant Graham Philpot's voice over the intercom. Usually imperturbable, the Vulcan's navigator-plotter sounded rattled.

"Our heading is one-twenty, target bearing two-fifteen. Offset is five nautical miles, range twenty-two and increasing!"

We're off course, thought Woodruff. Then again, armed with a one-megaton warhead, did it really matter?

"Roger," said Harrington. "Adjusting course to..."

As the Vulcan banked, an interjection from Freddie Jameson emphasised their predicament.

"Incoming, vector two-fifty, locked on."

Harrington pitched the Vulcan into a steep dive. Though designed to be flown like fighter, the Vulcan could not out-fly one. Its pilot would try, though.

"Let's go home," muttered Woodruff.

Graham Philpot came through on the intercom again.

"You reckon we've got homes to go back to?"

For once, Woodruff felt glad he'd never married.

"We have a present to deliver to Khrushchev," declared Harrington. He glanced at Woodruff. "Those are our orders." He paused to consult the instruments before passing the crucial instruction to Philpot.

"Flight, when you're ready."

Moments later, the Vulcan jerked like a man on the end of a rope. While he waited for the detonation, Woodruff fought an urge to pull back the blinds. The Yellow Sun warhead would outshine its namesake a thousand-fold. If he pressed the heel of his hand into his good eye, he would see the bones stark as an X-ray.

Watching the glow filter through the starboard blinds, Woodruff pondered whether their mission had achieved anything more than a futile redistribution of radioactive ashes. Harrington's grunt as he re-engaged the autopilot indicated no such qualms.

As they flew westwards, Woodruff pictured hundreds of mushroom clouds towering over Eastern Europe.

The debate about how to end the mission proved brief but bitter. In the unlikely event of returning from Warsaw Pact airspace, a Vulcan crew was supposed to land at a NATO airbase. Assuming any remained operational, Woodruff reminded himself. Harrington snorted when he suggested bailing out over Sweden.

"Boscombe Down was still open last I heard," said Philpot.

"Home it is then," agreed Harrington.

Shortly after the Vulcan's ground-following radar picked out the Dorset coastline, Woodruff peeled back the forward blinds. Looking ahead, he glimpsed the runway through a gap in the cloud layer.

"Cover your good eye," said Harrington.

Woodruff's reaction preceded the flash by a split-second.

"Alan, you have the controls. Flight, give him a heading for Filton."

We have one last chance, Woodruff realised, as he removed his eye-patch; but he had no time to set a new course before the shockwave hit. The aircraft pitched and rolled while he fought the stick. On finally regaining control, he told himself that he could fly a Vulcan after all. Making his first ever landing, with only one eye, would be quite a different matter, though.

With too little fuel for a go-around, he ordered the rear crew to bail out before he began the final descent.

The Vulcan rolled to a halt at the end of the runway, a few yards short of a greensward crisped by the explosion that had destroyed much of Bristol. Following Harrington's instructions to the tee, Woodruff had managed to bring the bomber down to a bone-jarring if ultimately safe landing.

He slapped his harness release and glanced at Harrington. His commander showed no signs of moving. He is blind, Woodruff reminded himself. But when he tried to assist, the Squadron Leader batted his hand away.

"Bring the survivors to me," he murmured.

What did Harrington intend? Woodruff could scarcely fly them out of Filton. In any case, fly them where? Khrushchev had clearly delivered on his promise to bomb Britain back into the Stone Age. Had the responsibility for dropping the bomb driven the Squadron Leader mad?

Woodruff wriggled out of the cockpit. Despite the risk from fallout, he did not plan to die cooped up in the Vulcan. Having lowered himself through the open hatch onto the tarmac, he gazed at the crater where hangers had once stood.

Flakes of ash fell from roiling clouds as Woodruff trotted along the runway. He lifted the film badge attached to his flight jacket. How large a dose had he absorbed during the mission? Probably not lethal, but the fallout's gamma radiation would soon make that question academic.

Woodruff knew he ought to hunker down in a shelter, like the government booklet advised, but "Protect and survive" seemed so much less truthful than "Mutually Assured Destruction". Instead of going to ground, he felt an absurd desire to walk upon it while he still had the chance.

He felt his guts heave before he found his first corpse.

By mid-morning, he had walked for miles and found dozens of corpses, some incinerated, others crushed by rubble. The world smelt of pulverised brick dust overlaid with the stench of scorched flesh.

Around midday, he heard a cry coming from a ruined bungalow. It took him two hours to rescue the girl. Though caught in the open, unlike her parents she had managed to crawl into the shelter before the blast wave hit. Second-degree burns covered most of her body and her hair had been burnt to fuzz. Superficially, the girl was not that badly injured, but now she faced a slow death from radiation poisoning. Woodruff thought about strangling her, but knew he lacked the courage. That she would not be able to watch him made no difference whatsoever.

Later, he found a ten-year-old boy, also blind, screaming for his mother as hobbled on a broken ankle. His clothes were in tatters, his face and chest horribly charred.

Feeling giddy and sick, Woodruff led his charges back to the Vulcan.

The children whimpered as Woodruff strapped them into the empty seats of the rear compartment. Moving forward into the cockpit, he found Harrington sitting in the pilot's seat, as if preparing for take-off.

"Good man," murmured the Squadron Leader, patting Woodruff's arm. "But there will be others."

Woodruff nodded.

As he staggered along the runway, he looked towards the zenith. A gap in the clouds revealed a fast-moving speck. The aircraft would doubtless photograph the Vulcan parked on the runway.

A line from a John Betjeman poem crept into his head. Harrington had read the situation right.

One friendly bomb would do.

STAR IN A GLASS

Curled up tight as an ammonite, Mira unwound in slow motion before leaping into the air with her limbs spread like a starfish. Bass notes thundered as her feet hit the floor, drawing a nod of approval from me.

Glancing at her mind's eye display, I saw a monstrous wave on the brink of rolling over—a credible match to her moves. Yet as she breast-stroked to the front of the stage, setting off ripples of percussion, her amplified vocals in no way resembled the powerful soprano of her downloads. Studio trickery had evidently worked wonders. But if she couldn't deliver the goods live, she was no use to Dusk 'til Dawn.

Dali delivered his verdict by killing the sound. Mira turned to me as I stepped out of the v-drum zone. I shook my head.

"Sorry love, the band needs a new singer, not a new drummer."

Drumming was my job; had been ever since Dusk 'til Dawn got started. Back then, Kerrang! ridiculed us as "Muse crossed with Led Zeppelin fronted by Amy Winehouse's bad sister, with added ballet." But we managed to build a huge fan-base, probably because we didn't sound like a bunch of Eighties throwbacks. Now, of course, we were just another prog-metal-ballet band (but hey, we were the first!) reforming for one last ride on the gravy train, or The Tour to End All Tours as our publicist dubbed it. But unless we could find a new singer-cum-dancer, we were going nowhere.

Mira gave me an imploring look, but I mouthed "sorry" before she could beg for another try.

"Well, fuck you then!" She plucked the ME reader from her forehead and threw it at me, just missing, before stomping off towards the nearest exit, her rainbow dreadlocks shaking like wheat in a gale.

Cute arse, decent head-stuff and some competent incidental percussion, I said to myself, but the voice wasn't a patch on Diva's.

I turned round to find Dali looming over me like a Bronte hero crossed with a praying mantis. He ran lace-clad fingers through lank, shoulder-length hair before prodding me in the chest. Tattoos flickered over his exquisitely chiselled cheekbones, coding for some emotional state I couldn't quite figure.

"Toad, this was your goddam idea!"

"Toad" as in short, fat and ugly: the warty guy standing at the back, pounding four-four out of thin air like the Devil's own blacksmith while Dali conjured up the frills and flourishes. But the band needed a soul, not just its head and heart. And in Dusk 'til Dawn's case that meant Diva. No way could some wannabe rock-chick fresh out of art school fill her thigh-length boots.

"True," I said, "but you signed on the dotted line."

"I should've known better!"

I shrugged but said nothing. We were in this together; Dali knew that.

"Okay," he said, "so who else have you got lined up?"

I punched his chest, but gently, like we were two mates joshing. "You know, I could fix our problem, if you'd just let me try."

Dali knew precisely what I meant and it got to him precisely how I intended.

"No way!" Dali said, his mirrored eyes blazing. "No bloody way does that woman sneak back into my band!"

"Our band."

"Whatever!"

"So, do we pull out of the tour?"

I picked the dirt out of my fingernails while waiting for Dali to cave in, which I knew he would 'cos he hated the vanilla life, same as I did. Sure, he'd carved out a lucrative niche building gizmos for the Music Industry—the mind's eye reader was his latest invention—but backroom boys don't get the acclaim, hence his willingness to reform the band.

Dali sighed his acquiescence. "Okay, do it your way, but tell me, how long is it since anyone actually clapped eyes on her?"

"Five years, give or take."

Dali shook his head like he thought the project was doomed from the start.

"Even if she hasn't flat-lined, she'll have stealthed herself to the max. You'll never distinguish her from a JoPub."

Relieved that I'd worked a chink in Dali's armour, I offered him an inducement.

"Then I'll need your help, won't I?"

I've always known how to appeal to his vanity.

"Okay, Toad," Dali said with a sigh. "Go fetch."

But first find.

After squandering enough carbon credits to ensure boredom wasn't my only reason for reforming the band, a third-hand rumour saw me fly into LA.

The woman leaning over a toilet bowl in Bar Fusion's rest-room didn't look much like Diva, what with the razor-bobbed platinum hairdo, Nordic cheekbones and big tits, but Dali's latest gizmo had confirmed her identity shortly after I fed it a sample of her saliva.

"Hello, Diva."

She turned her head and blinked at me. "Huh?"

I couldn't tell whether she'd had her voice re-coded, but right now the fact that her eyes were focused some place north of nowhere concerned me more. So I tugged her upright and frog-marched her into the bar. She slumped over the counter, resting her head on her arms.

"What'll it be?"

The bartender was resting his forearms on the aquarium counter-top, his biceps bulging like lotto balls in a silk bag. He looked so what's-his-face the surgery must have cost a fortune.

I grabbed a menu. Gaining Diva's cooperation meant getting on her wavelength, which meant taking the same drugs, only not quite as many. I scrolled through the list of cocktails, all of them unfamiliar to me. So what was it to be, a Rigel or an Antares, a Sirius or a Betelgeuse? An Omicron what, for Odin's sake?

Biceps grinned at me in a way doubtless meant to encourage the uninitiated. "I'd start with a Sol, if I were you."

Before I could ask what went into one of those, Diva elbowed me in the ribs. "Wanna try an Albeiro."

The words were slurred but her voice sounded sultry, imperious, irresistible—just like the Diva of old.

Biceps blinked up a holo-tab. "You don't have the credit, doll."

Diva turned to me, eyes flaring wide. "Pay the man, Toad."

Biceps grinned like a rattlesnake eyeing its prey. I held out my right hand, jerked it back the instant I felt the confirmatory tingle. The man possessed a clammy grip.

"Got somewhere private?" I asked, quickly adding: "Just me and the girl."

Biceps indicated a door opposite the rest-room. "Booth Five, through there. Make yourselves comfortable while I fix your Albeiro."

I imagined a Victorian opium den. Bar Fusion's update on the theme didn't disappoint. After settling Diva on the mouth-shaped couch, I patched in the data-link to Dali. Moments later, Biceps appeared holding a tray of coloured ampoules and a transparent cocktail shaker. He placed the equipment on the aquarium table with a gentleness that suggested a replacement might be hard to find. After pouring the contents of two ampoules into the jug, he flicked a toggle switch on its base. The teeth-jarring vibration caused the table's aquatic residents to scatter. The mixture frothed into a creamy fog. Biceps tapped his remote control, plunging the booth into darkness.

Twin sparks flared inside the cocktail shaker, one golden-hued the other eggshell blue, both dazzlingly bright. Peering through a fence of fingers, I counted to ten before the sparks winked out.

"Okay," I said, all low and slow, impressed but nervous too.

Biceps whispered the booth's lights up a notch so I could see him pour the mix into a pair of shot glasses. After taking hers, Diva cuddled up to me, which made me tremble for more than one reason. That's unrequited love for you, I guess.

"This one's for you, Diva," I said.

We clinked glasses and downed our shots.

The cocktail hit low, mean and dirty. It felt like I had a chili-coated spider scuttling around my stomach. Sweat beaded my face. I gulped down hard as bile surged up my throat.

The bartender leaned over the table and chuckled.

"Now, close your—"

In my mind's eye I saw a sphere of blue-green incandescence. Hot and brilliant, dazzling and dangerous, the star in my head shone on me, only me. But I was a star too, bigger and brighter than my companion. I bathed her with my golden rays. We loved each other with our light.

Wow, like fucking wow!

I could have worshipped that star forever.

"Time to wake up, Toad."

Dali's prompting sounded urgent, but I felt too nauseous to respond, so I tongue-clicked the link to "off". I blinked open gummy eyes, but closed them again on seeing the booth's walls revolve. I vomited, narrowly missing the aquarium table. After wiping my mouth on the back of my hand, I glanced at my wristwatch tattoo. An hour had passed.

Wow, I thought. That really was a stellar head-fuck-and-a-half.

Feeling weak as a new-born, I lay back on the sofa and gazed at Diva. Her remodelled features looked relaxed and serene, her cheeks held some colour. She definitely looked better than when I'd found her. Was that a side effect of the drug?

"How're you doing?" I asked when her eyelids fluttered open.

Diva rocked her head to indicate "not so bad". A moment later her grimace dissolved into a wicked grin. "So, now you've broken your duck, how about trying another?"

I shook my head, well aware that I couldn't match her legendary stamina. Instead, I tongue-clicked the link back on.

"About bloody time!" Dali's voice fizzed with anger.

"Okay, we're out of here."

As I helped Diva out of the booth, I thanked Odin that I'd never managed to get myself addicted to anything genuinely harmful. Granted, I'd enjoyed satisfying the usual rock-star appetites, but unlike Diva I'd always known when to say "no".

"Poor, self-deluding Toad," Dali said, as if he'd read my mind. I wanted to yell "You hateful shit" back at him but thought better of it. Now more than ever, I needed him on my side. So instead I settled for, "I could use some help here!"

"Just bring her home," Dali said, sounding resigned. "I've cleared things with the authorities."

"Got to fly," I said to Biceps as I hustled Diva towards the exit.

"Pity you can't stay," he said, grinning so solicitously I wanted to punch him. "I have this amazing...."

I shook my head. And punched him anyway.

Two weeks after flying back into London, I delivered a transformed but only superficially cleaned-up Diva to Dali's rehearsal space. One glance at his face while he sized her up was enough to tell me that a storm was brewing.

As for me, well I tried not to drool. Those violet-flecked eyes, the milk chocolate skin, that jet-black hair falling all the way to her skinny backside.... Diva's retrofit had cost me a small fortune, but I reckoned the results easily justified the outlay. She looked stunning, wrong side of forty or not.

Frowning, Dali turned to me. "Is she ready to audition?"

Diva snarled a vicious obscenity and flounced off-stage, trailing finger gestures that left nothing to the imagination.

I gaped at Dali. "For fuck's sake, you don't audition Diva!"

"Why not?"

I grabbed his chin with my left hand and tugged real hard, so that he bent his knees. With our eyes now level, I said, "You just don't, right?"

He jerked his head free. "I honestly hoped you wouldn't find her."

To be frank, I could see where he was coming from. Watching Diva blow her talent first time around had been hard enough for me, but so much worse for Dali, because while I'd lusted at her from afar he'd been her lover for real. Still, retrieving Diva had cost me a lot of time and money, so I wasn't about to let Dali squirm out of our agreement.

"Just give her a chance," I said.

"But she's still an addict!"

I wasn't about to argue with him having spent a fortnight fending off a legion of pushers.

"I can sort her out," I said.

Dali gave me a pitying look. "Do you know anything about this new shit she's into?"

"No," I said, certain that I'd get a lecture from him whether I wanted one or not.

"Ever heard of sonoluminescence?"

"Sono-what?"

Dali fired up TrustWiki on the nearest screen. "See for yourself."

So I did.

Sonoluminescence: the light radiated by a bubble of gas when compressed by an isotropic supersonic sound wave.

"Otherwise known as the star in a glass," Dali said over my shoulder.

I kept reading.

Back in 2002, a physicist named Taleyarkhan had claimed that his sonoluminescence experiments proved the existence of cold fusion. The techie rags briefly got all frothy at the prospect of cheap, clean energy in a bottle, but those scientists who repeated his experiments failed to detect the excess neutrons that would have proved Taleyarkhan's hypothesis. Despite his protestations, the verdict was "fairy tale" not "fusion".

So how had a mere bartender managed to obtain the sono-shaker kit? His cocktails had generated a fair bit of comment in the blogosphere, but I could find no evidence of a commercial supplier. The consensus was "grad student prank".

Dali chuckled evilly in my right ear. "Anyone Jacko enough to drink the by-products of a failed lab experiment deserves to get their head sunburnt on the inside."

He meant Diva, of course, but I'd glimpsed that fat old sun too. How long, I wondered, before I needed another fix?

I gave Dali a look that I hoped was argument-proof.

"One chance, that's all she needs."

Dali's nod was a long time coming.

Diva stood centre-stage, her fingers tickling wind chimes out of thin air. Twenty years after we'd last played it, the opening to Snowbound sounded wondrously spectral, but when Dali cued up Diva's vocal with a flourish of church organ she sang the first notes so flat it hurt. With a sigh of despair, she sank to the floor. The bass generator rumbled like indigestion.

"This is hopeless," she said.

I sighed inwardly. If Diva couldn't sing Snowbound then Dusk 'til Dawn was in deep trouble, 'cos that was one of our simplest pieces.

Dali fired up Diva's ME display. The screen showed a solitary star: small and white. It faded perceptibly while I watched.

Dali's voice crackled in my earpiece. "Yeah, that figures."

"How do you mean?"

"From a cosmic standpoint, she's a white dwarf."

I didn't recognise the term but I assumed he meant a burnt-out case, in which case his verdict was hard to refute. If we'd had ME-tech fifteen years ago, Diva's inner star would surely have shone brighter than the Tehran Nuke.

As Dali emerged from behind his nest of keyboards, I glanced at Diva, who was only now getting to her feet. She squared her shoulders in a display of self-possession.

"I could try again," she said.

Dali snorted derisively. "Please don't bother!"

Diva turned to me, her expression ferocious. "Thanks for nothing, Toad."

I stared at my warty hands, ashamed that I had coerced Diva to "audition" before her unforgiving ex-lover.

Dali shouted "Timewaster!" as she stomped off stage. I shot him a look almost as vicious as Diva's.

"Any chance you could shut it while I sort this out?"

I ignored his muttered reply.

I gave Diva a few minutes to compose herself before I entered her dressing room, where I found her staring blankly at the mirror. It was obvious she needed another fix—and soon. As I had no intention of sending her back to LA, I'd have to find a local source of the drug. If only I'd had the foresight to steal the cocktail kit from Bar Fusion I wouldn't now have to persuade Dali to construct a home-grown version. But he would demand a cast iron guarantee that Dusk 'til Dawn would get back on track in time for the tour. But that meant sorting out Diva, which meant....

My mind reeled with the circularity of it all.

Diva's drug habit lay at the heart of our problem, but might it not also offer a solution? After all, the double cocktail we had shared in Bar Fusion had definitely made her feel better, if only briefly. And hadn't Biceps hinted at the existence of even more potent concoctions?

Convinced that I finally had a fix on how to get Diva's mojo rising again, I trotted back to the stage, where Dali had begun packing up. He tried to shrug me off, but I had him cornered.

"What if I guarantee to get Diva sorted out?"

Dali closed his eyes and shook his head, like we'd had this conversation a dozen times before, which was close enough true.

"She's no bloody use to herself, never mind us. She'd rather die than do detox." Dali had never majored in forgiveness and it didn't sound like he planned to change his ways now.

"In that case we have to exploit her addiction."

Dali's forehead furrowed, which I took to be a good sign. "And how do you propose to do that?"

"Remember what it was like before we made it big? How we used to share everything: our digs, our money, even our drugs?"

Back then we'd lived in each other's pockets, just so we could make it to the next stop on the toilet circuit. Now, twenty years on, we'd have to learn how to share everything again. I took a deep breath and explained my plan.

When I finished, he said, "It's risky as hell."

"It's my risk to take," I said. "But I'll need you to build the sono-shaker."

The gleam in Dali's eyes confirmed my ploy had worked. I thanked Odin that I'd asked Dali to collect data from Bar Fusion while I collected Diva.

"Okay, give me a week and I'll replicate the kit for you." Dali's grin set a new benchmark for smug. "Just let me know what ingredients you need."

But that was the problem, 'cos I didn't know yet. Decrypting the bartender's recipes would be child's play for Dali, but I didn't relish the prospect of sampling every one of them while searching for Diva's sweet spot. That would really do my head in.

So instead, I decided to learn more about stars.

Reading TrustWiki's article on stellar evolution, I discovered that the Sun will play nicely for another billion years, before it bloats into a red giant and fries whatever vermin outlive Humanity. After that, it'll shed its outer layers like an old suit, leaving behind a nub of star-stuff growing cold. A white dwarf: the star that's dead but doesn't know it yet.

Just like Diva.

But that's not necessarily the end, 'cos if a white dwarf orbits a bloated companion, its gravity can sometimes steal enough star-stuff to generate a nuclear flash. The huge outpouring of energy makes the dying star shine brightly again, for a while.

So, could I make Diva go nova?

I puffed out my chest and paradiddled the air with my fists. Virtual tom-toms rattled the stage like an earthquake. Fat old Toad still had energy to spare.

Grinning like a fool, I began cross-referencing Dali's decrypt of the bartender's recipes with TrustWiki's descriptions of star-types. My search for the perfect cocktail took a while, but eventually I found a match.

Yes, a shot of RS Ophiuchi ought to do the trick.

One week later, as promised, Dali unboxed his version of the sono-shaker.

"Will it work?" I asked, frowning at the bulky-looking device.

Dali rolled his eyes. "Of course it'll bloody work!"

I asked the question not because I doubted his engineering skills, but rather that his sono-shaker's by-products presumably remained un-tested,

Dali having given up drugs shortly after Dusk 'til Dawn hit the Big Time. Indeed, it was a furious row sparked by Diva playing under the influence that heralded the band's break-up. Knowing that I couldn't avoid a lecture from Dali on the subject, I decided to pre-empt it by feigning curiosity.

"So, have you figured out how the drug works?"

Dali grinned like a pub bore invited to expound on his pet subject. "The cocktail you consumed in LA was a twin-payload sono-drug. The first component boosts the empathic centre of your brain, while the second makes you sweat so much that a pheromone-mediated pathway is established." My frown forced Dali into hand-waving simplification. "In layman's terms: the drug opens a channel that allows the transfer of mental energy."

"Which only works one-way," I said, recalling my Bar Fusion experience.

Dali shrugged. "I suppose some people are suppliers and others consumers." He paused, presumably to let me ponder the implications. "Still want to proceed?"

I nodded.

Dali glanced at Diva. She was sitting cross-legged on the floor, facing away from him. "Is she ready?"

I sat down beside her, gave her leather-clad left knee a squeeze. "How about trying Fire in the Deep?"

Dali whistled. With good reason, 'cos Fire was the most complicated piece on our set-list: the track that earned us the 'prog-metal-ballet' tag. If Diva could perform it, we'd be on to something; if not, then no one would pay to see us.

"I can do this," she said, seemingly for her own benefit rather than Dali's or mine.

With a little help from me, I said to myself. That, plus the venue's air-conditioning set to sauna-like levels. I was sweating already.

While Diva began mapping out her dance moves, I double-checked the RS Ophiuchi recipe. Satisfied that I had it right, I tore open the ampoules and poured their contents into the shaker. After receiving a nod from Dali, I flicked the switch on its base. On the count of three, twin sparks of red and white flared. When they guttered out, I poured the contents of the shaker into two shot glasses. Dali began playing Fire's opening riff.

Standing centre-stage, Diva tipped her head so that her hair veiled her face. Her fingers fluttered while Dali's organ chords rolled over us like the aftermath of the Big Bang. As the overture faded, Diva flicked a smile at me. I handed her a glass, which she clinked against mine. We downed our shots together. Chili heat seeped from my every pore, this time without the side-order of nausea. After slinging my glass, I gave Diva a hug that should have got me arrested. Our sweat mingled. Finally, regretfully, I let go of her, closed my eyes and began pummelling the air with my fists.

Inside my head, I saw a feeble, pallid, dying star. What Diva needed was a jolly red giant: fat old Toad radiating his life force. I felt the light pouring out of me. Here Diva, take a piece of me, I said to myself, shaking beads of sweat from my body while I drove Fire in the Deep forward.

To my relief, I saw Diva's star brighten as she started singing the first verse. Her voice sounded clear and true.

"Fire in the deep, adrift in your zone.

Stars in your eyes, love in my own.

Destined to fly, lest Humanity die,

Singing of freedom and home."

I paradiddled like John Bonham, propelling the song towards its climax, which Dali heralded with a typically bombastic fanfare. As the electronic storm faded towards ambient, Diva began singing her a capella section, but she sliced the high notes horribly before stuttering into silence. Inside my mind, I watched her star fade.

When I opened my eyes I saw Diva standing with her head lowered; a mute witness to a stupid plan.

Dali strode across the stage towards me, waggling his forefinger like an irate schoolteacher. "I told you so!"

"It was worth a try, dammit!"

"No, it fucking wasn't!"

I raised my fists. Thumping Dali wouldn't help Diva, but I'd feel better. He took a step back, then another. I followed him.

"We're a trio, dammit!"

That was Diva. I turned to face her, likewise Dali. She stood before us, her eyes burning with accusation.

"What?" Dali and I said in unison.

"We're supposed to be a trio!" Her voice dripped accusation.

Dali kicked Diva's discarded glass across the stage. "I've had enough of this farce," he said, turning his back on Diva – and the band too, or so I feared.

"Wait!"

"What now?"

"Come on, Dali. You have to admit we were a bit untogether just now."

Dali rolled his eyes. "It's Diva who's untogether!"

"That's rich coming from you!" Diva jabbed a forefinger at Dali's chest. "Were you deliberately trying to put me off or what?"

I let them snarl at each other while I tried to figure out what had gone wrong. Thinking back, it felt like we'd been too busy doing our own thing to feed on each other's inspiration. To conjure up the old musical alchemy we would have to play for each other, which meant that Dali would really have to join in—and not just musically.

I stepped between my warring band-mates. "What we need," I said, "is a treble."

Dali shook his head. "No—fucking—way!"

I gave him my fiercest look, 'cos I wasn't about to let him off the hook. I waved away his protests while flicking through the recipe book in search of a suitable cocktail.

When we resumed rehearsals, I made sure I was calling the shots not just pouring them. I placed a glass on top of Dali's Hammond organ and pushed it towards him. His scowl could have struck sparks from a bar of soap.

"Just drink it!" I said.

Dali shook his head. "No chance."

I followed him into his keyboard-filled sanctum, which provoked the intended look of horror. Doing my usual looming-from-below thing, I poked his chest good and hard. He recoiled but could not escape.

"Look, we both need this to work," I said, "'cos without Diva, we're done. What's more, if you don't help me sort out Diva, you'll need a new drummer." I grabbed Dali's portable Roland, which he rarely used, and dangled it from the strap. "Come on, we need you on stage!"

My heart skipped a beat when Dali picked up the glass and sloshed the contents, then threatened to stop working altogether when he put it back un-drained. I gave him a stare and turned away. There was still time.

"The guy's a prick," I said to Diva, loudly enough for Dali to hear. She whispered "Thanks for trying" before sinking her own shot. I followed suit, gritting my teeth against the burn while reaching for Diva. She felt hot and slippery in my arms. When I released her I stepped back just enough to give her room to dance, while ensuring we would spatter each other with our sweat. I began hammering out the beat to Fire in the Deep.

In my mind's eye I saw a single star, floating in the blackness. I radiated crimson rays towards my companion while trying to re-direct my trajectory towards her.

But for all my exertions, Diva's vocals quavered when they should have soared. And Dali's prissy keyboard fills weren't helping one bit. Second time around was panning out no better than the first—and I knew Dali wouldn't give her another chance.

So I flipped up my lip-microphone and said, "Dali, you're a selfish, arrogant, son-of-a..."

New light burst in my head: dazzling, brilliant, eye-searingly blue.

Dali was a star!

Big Blue flashed past me ripping out gouts of star-stuff that spiralled towards my companion. I looked on in awe as Diva flared so bright she outshone Dali, never mind me.

Now, at last, Diva sang with the power of old. Her voice soared and swooped, every note pitch-perfect, every drop of emotion wrung from her soul, while Dali fired off riffs that rolled over the stage like a tsunami. This was how Fire in the Deep was supposed to sound!

I opened my eyes. Dali was standing between Diva and me, grinning like a madman while conjuring cosmos-shaking sounds from his Roland. My arms felt heavy as logs, but I pummelled the air with all the energy I could muster.

During one of the quieter passages, I sneaked a glance at Diva's mind's eye display. The screen showed three stars dancing an orbital ballet: a pair of bobby-dazzlers accompanied by a dull red giant.

As Fire in the Deep's coda faded towards ambient, I swung my left fist to close out the piece with the sound of a gong. When the echoes had died down, I glanced at Diva. She was sitting on her heels with her arms wrapped around her knees. Her shoulders were shaking, but whether from exertion or the release of pent-up emotion, I couldn't tell.

What happened next made my jaw drop. I hadn't expected Dali to acknowledge Diva's performance with more than a cursory nod. Instead, he knelt down beside her, whispered something in her ear and helped her to her feet. But it was the passionate embrace that shocked me. The band appeared to be reforming in more ways than one. I wasn't too sure how I felt about that.

"Diva, that was amazing," Dali said as he released her. But the look he gave me was kind of distant.

We rehearsed three more songs that day. Diva played a blinder, superbly accompanied by Dali. As for me, well, the band had got its soul back, and its head had never stopped working, but the heart wasn't pumping like it should. Fuelling Diva's nova had burned me out. She knew it—and judging by his expression, so did Dali.

As I packed away my drum lasers, Dali manoeuvred Diva to one side. I didn't hear what either of them said, but I could read her lips.

Okay, I'll tell him.

Diva walked over and gave me a hug. "I'm so, so sorry, dearest Toad," she said, her voice muffled by my shoulder, "but we need to bring in someone younger."

She somehow managed to make rejection seem like a kindness.

The next two days passed in a blur. I began by drinking a crate of beer and followed up with a couple of bottles of Jack. When I finally sobered up enough to return to the rehearsal hall, intending only to collect my equipment, what I saw made Dali hugging Diva seem like the most predictable event in the history of music.

Dusk 'til Dawn was rehearsing as a trio, with Mira, the dreadlocked wannabe who had failed to emulate Diva, filling in for me. Like me, Dali had observed that she could play virtual percussion. Unlike me, he had considered how he could make use of that talent.

After I got over the shock, which took most of the band's run-through of Snowbound, it occurred to me that there was one thing Mira didn't know how do—and that was how to keep Diva fuelled and flaring. Having exhausted me, Diva would soon need a top-up.

Unnoticed by the band, I made my way back-stage and grabbed the cocktail shaker. As I ran out in front of Mira, the music faltered. She looked aghast. Diva's expression mixed pity with irritation, whereas Dali didn't acknowledge my presence at all. Shaking with anger, I stomped over to his eyrie, accompanied by a series of juddering bass notes, and hurled the shaker to the floor. It shattered into a satisfyingly large number of pieces.

Dali sighed. "I can replace that too, you know."

I nodded. "Sure you can, but I'd start now if I were you, 'cos I've learnt enough astrophysics to know that a nova fades once it has exhausted its fuel." I waved a fistful of ampoules under his nose. "I reckon the sono-drug 'trip' works in exactly the same way. So Diva will burn brightly, just not for very long."

She'd begin by feeding off Mira, I reckoned, but sooner rather than later she'd turn to Dali, which would kill Dusk 'til Dawn, 'cos you can replace a band's heart, as I'd found out the hard way, but not its head. So, if she couldn't live off the band that just left the fans. It seemed we needed them every bit as much as they needed us; more, if anything.

I stood on tiptoe, reached over Dali's keyboard stack and slapped him on both shoulders. "Dali my old mate, I reckon you're gonna need a much bigger cocktail shaker."

His expression would have slaughtered Mira, but was no match for Toad. When Dali looked to Diva for support she responded with a shrug.

"He's right, you know."

And that is how I became Dusk 'til Dawn's road manager.

If the Kyoto gig hadn't been the opening night of the tour, I'd have cancelled as soon as I saw the advance sales, 'cos playing to a half-empty hall usually spells doom for a rock band. To justify continuing we'd need to generate some awesome word-of-mouth. So I took a leaf out of Dali's book and prepared accordingly, with the result that every punter who bought the band's merchandise received a complementary squeeze-tube of sono-cocktail.

"Yes, sir—" In my mind, I bowed politely, imitating the counter staff, "—you can take your drink into the hall. But don't try to open it yet, because the tear-strip is word-locked."

I'd tested that particular feature to my satisfaction, but the same couldn't be said for the sono-drug. To improve the odds that Praesepe would work, I'd arranged to have the balcony closed. With the air-conditioning turned off, the JoPubs would swelter in the mosh pit.

Watching the band walk out onto the stage I felt a pang of regret though not of jealousy. Mira had proved herself a highly capable v-drummer—and it no longer hurt me to admit it. Better still, she looked the part: youthful, confident and brimming with energy. I particularly liked the fact that she shared a name with a star. Unlike her celestial counterpart our Mira showed no signs of extreme variability.

If only the same could be said of Diva. She stood centre-stage with her head bowed, her hair veiling the fearful look I'd seen in her eyes. She knew full well whose performance would make or break the tour.

Feeling no less jittery, I took a deep breath and followed the trio out onto the stage. A single spotlight picked me out as I strode forward.

"Kyoto, are you ready to ROCK?"

That drew a muted roar of approval but not a single chant of "We want Toad!"

How quickly the fans forgot.

I held up a squeeze-tube. "Kyoto, are you ready to DRINK?" This time the yells were deafening.

Holographic numerals floated above the stage as I began the countdown. The JoPubs counted with me, many in English. A communally roared "Zero!" was the cue for everyone to tear open their squeeze-tubes. I swigged my shot while running to the side of the stage. Dali began soundscaping and I closed my eyes.

The light from a myriad stars blazed inside my head. Brightest of all was a triple star system comprising the familiar combo of blue giant and white dwarf, but now escorted by a pretty yellow companion. I orbited further out, separating the trio from the remainder of the cluster.

Mira began hammering her virtual tom-toms as if punishing the air that we breathed, while Dali jabbed organ notes that made my guts vibrate. But as Diva began singing the first verse of Snowbound, her voice wavered. She continued to muff the high notes throughout the song. As Snowbound petered out into sonic sleet, I heard a smattering of boos.

I opened my eyes and glanced at Dali, who responded with a tight-lipped nod. As he began playing the opening chords of Fire in the Deep, I muttered a prayer to Odin, ran to the edge of the stage and belly-flopped onto a sea of raised hands. Surfing the mosh pit, I harvested the fans' sweat, energy and adoration, heedless of the cuts and bruises inflicted on me. While in my mind's eye, I navigated a sea of stars, gaining energy from each encounter, while gradually following a trajectory back to the triple system.

A glancing blow to my head forced me to open my eyes. I saw Mira waving at me, splashing virtual cymbals into Dali's live mix.

Come on, she mouthed. Join us!

The fans at the front of the mosh pit roared: "We want Toad!" as I clambered onto the stage. I grinned as Mira made room for me. I took over on virtual drums while she danced a bass line, stamping out notes with her bare feet. Our partnership worked perfectly, driving Dali to even greater heights of virtuosity. He danced around the stage, dabbing sampled guitar riffs from his keyboard. The air felt sticky with sweat: Mira's and mine, Dali's and Diva's. I closed my eyes.

After re-establishing my celestial bearings, I performed a slingshot manoeuvre around Diva's companions and settled into orbit around her. Gravity immediately began stripping me of my star-stuff. Yet, despite the intensity of Diva's hunger I felt no fear. I would gladly have given all of me to see her flare into life again. But would all of me be enough?

Just as my flow began to fail, I witnessed a burst of light so brilliant it made the rest of the star cluster look like fireflies. Overwhelmed by Diva's luminosity, I opened my eyes, blinking until my vision cleared.

Now, at last, Diva really sang. She pitched her voice so high it seemed to bounce off the mirrorball, growled so low she was molesting Mira's bass line. And did she ever dance! To see her pirouette for the first time in fifteen years, her elbows firing off salvos of incidental percussion ... well, tears trickled down my cheeks, that's for sure.

As we brought Fire in the Deep to a close, a thousand JoPubs erupted with the loudest applause I'd ever heard. The stage invasion during the encore was the icing on the cake.

Needless to say, we got some awesome word-of-mouth.

.

When Dusk 'til Dawn set out on The Tour to End All Tours, we didn't expect to finish with five nights at The Brixton Academy, never mind that the final gig would climax with one of those "Where were you when...?" moments.

How terrible, then, that it was a moment of pure horror.

By the time we commenced the UK leg of the tour, we had ploughed the profits from merchandising into a whole lotta ME-tech. We installed screens everywhere: behind the stage, along the sidewalls and balcony, suspended from the gantries. Dali had decided to let our fans drive the visuals. Before every gig we handed out headsets to a couple of dozen lucky competition winners. Most newbies didn't generate anything better than psychedelic noise, so we let them carry sponsor vids as well. Kudos to those JoPubs who hacked the news-feeds, though! Even Dali was impressed.

Best of all, I no longer had to stoke up Diva. Fuelled with my latest sono-cocktail, which I'd christened Messier 13, she could feed off the crowd's euphoria without my help. But I still took a swig when Dali started playing the intro to Fire in the Deep. My crowd surfing had become an established part of our act.

The stars in my head sure looked bright that night. Little did I know that even Diva was about to be eclipsed.

After Security helped me back onto the stage, I looked out over the mosh pit and raised my fists in triumph. I was about to resume pounding my v-drums when eye-searing incandescence flooded the hall, like someone had collected the light from every supernova since the dawn of time and beamed it straight into the Academy. I stood there and gawped, the music forgotten.

The screams began in the mosh pit and spread like wildfire. Within seconds every phone, every screen, was showing vid-streams of the LA Nuke. Diva was the last to hear what had happened. When Dali whispered in her ear, she sank to her knees and wept.

As for me, I felt a pang of relief that I hadn't sent her back to Bar Fusion.

Needless to say, Dame Amy Winehouse and her mates organised a series of charity concerts for the survivors. It took a bit of arm-twisting, but I got Dusk 'til Dawn added to the line-up for Wembley. A mid-afternoon slot wasn't so great, but we made the best of it. We played a shorter set than usual, but didn't compromise on the sono-fusion stuff. It's what our fans had come to expect—and it's our fans that have kept us going.

Dali wrote a new song called Stoned Cold Fusion, which we debuted at the gig. I dedicated it to the LA barman with the big biceps.

I figured we owed him one.

DARK, THEY WERE, AND STRANGE INSIDE

If it weren't for the boffins who resurrected the Large Hadron Collider I wouldn't be placing flowers on my best friend's grave. For once, Marcie followed my advice. I wish she hadn't.

Marcie's journey to the hereafter began when she leaned across my kitchen table and fixed me with the kind of look she usually reserves for guys with performance issues.

"You did what?"

"I signed up for Internet dating!"

"Why'd you do that, Jen?"

"Cos I'm thirty-five."

Marcie rolled her eyes. "You're just having a cold spell. Everyone gets those."

Excepting Marcie, of course. She's never had to go shopping to get men. Big boobs and Beyoncé hair do the job for her, whereas I rate as presentable in a good light. Admittedly, I did select Attractive on the web-form, but then who wouldn't?

"Okay," Marcie said with a sigh. "Let's take a look."

I fired up my laptop. Marcie chuckled her way through the website's blurb.

"'Fundamentals.com: your portal to a multiverse of love.' Yeah, right!"

I scrolled through my profile, highlighting those difficult-to-write personal bits. Marcie waved me onwards.

"Never mind that drivel. What about your ideal man?"

I showed her.

"I see you've selected Dark."

"So?"

"I'm just saying." Her expression suggested she remembered my adventures with Ahmed.

"I did also select Attractive and Solvent."

"Which will get you Tubby and Tightwad." Marcie shook her head before giving me a wink. "Go for it girl!"

"So, you gonna tell me what happened?"

I could tell Marcie was excited because she didn't make her usual crack about Botox even though I was frowning.

"Well, I turned up at All Bar One wearing my—"

"I know what you were wearing!"

I blushed but said nothing.

"What did he look like?"

"It's hard to say."

Marcie groaned. "You did pick one with a photo, right?"

I shook my head. "No, but..."

"Have I taught you nothing?"

Quite the opposite in fact, but I wasn't about to say so. I sighed and continued my account.

"There were lots of men there, but no standalones. So I sat at a corner table and waited. After half an hour of cooling my heels, I was about to go when...the best way I can put it is that I felt a presence. I couldn't see him properly or work out what he was saying; yet I knew someone was sat next to me. But take it from me, you feel a right fool talking to thin air, so pretty soon I made my excuses and left."

"Good call."

"But walking to the bus-stop, I could feel someone holding my hand. And when I finally got into bed, well..."

"Omigod, you pulled!" Marcie high-fived me before asking the inevitable question: "So, was he any good?"

"Well, I did enjoy a very nice buzz."

I could tell Marcie wasn't convinced by the way she frowned at me. And who could blame her? But I knew I'd been to bed with a man, even if I hadn't actually clapped eyes on him at any stage.

I sipped my Chardonnay in silence while I awaited Marcie's verdict. Finally she delivered it.

"I bet he wasn't even dark, never mind tall and handsome."

On that point she couldn't have been more wrong.

The official news about our exotic friends broke the next day.

According to the hot-looking guy on Sky News, the Large Haddock Colander (the pride of CERN, as re-christened by Marcie) hadn't opened up a planet-swallowing black hole as some had predicted, but it had definitely opened up a gateway to something. Within days, an MIT boffin announced that he'd built a dark matter delineator. Once the portable model hit the stores, my dates got a lot easier to spot. Fortunately I've always preferred the silent type.

I was dating my fourth dark guy by the time Marcie decided to join in the fun. My best friend asking me for dating advice; now that was a first!

"Okay, let's build your profile," I said. "And no, you can't upload those photos of you wearing nothing."

Marcie waggled her tongue at me before clicking her way through the options so expertly I wondered whether she was quite as inexperienced at this kind of thing as she claimed.

"I see you didn't select Dark," I said.

Marcie grinned like a snake hypnotising a mouse.

"I'm looking for something a lot stronger than a 'very nice buzz'!"

After three days with no phone calls or messages, I felt sick with worry. I texted Marcie a lurid description of my latest date, but didn't receive a reply. Either she was having such a good time it had left her speechless— another first—or her alley-cat morals had finally landed her in trouble.

As I drove into Marcie's street a fleet of fire engines and ambulances wailed past. Some hundred metres from her home, a police-boy with a volcanic complexion waved me back. He needn't have bothered. One glance at the huge pile of smoking rubble where Marcie's apartment block had once stood was enough.

Last I heard the death toll had topped 50. Needless to say, Fundamentals.com has withdrawn its Energetic option. It seems that some guys really are too dangerous to date, especially those made of antimatter. According to the boffins, the containment field needs more work.

Once the dust has settled I'll resume dating. Marcie would want me to. I miss her terribly but remember her well. Say what you like about my best friend, but she definitely went out with a bang.

SURVIVAL STRATEGIES

Shrouded in darkness, I wait for the Egg to release me. After what seems like an eternity, a coin of creamy light appears before my eyes. A familiar voice whispers in my ear, urging me onwards. I focus on the disk; try to grasp it with my mind. It flows towards me, expanding all the while, until I am enveloped in a panorama of black, white and grey.

At first the wrap-around image fails to keep pace with my movements, but within seconds the drugs fed to me by the Egg begin to mitigate the effects of irreducible distance. Prediction and perception bind together in a chemical embrace, concealing the delay between cause and effect. Time-lagged there transforms into virtual here as unreal time takes hold.

I am telepresent on the surface of the Moon, rolling across the landscape on wheels of aluminium. Though my body languishes in an Earth-side isolation chamber, cobwebbed with sensors, my viewpoint is that of a geological survey robot roving the lunar *maria*. The Terabit network link restrains my freedom like an electronic leash. It is an ever-present reminder that the work I perform is intended as a punishment.

As I prospect for rare minerals in the lunar soil, the passing seconds rush me inexorably towards snatch-back.

The Egg retrieves me.

Reverse lag, where my actions seem to precede my thoughts, confuses me for a few seconds, but the sensation ebbs away as a further dose of drugs reintegrates my mind into Egg-time, removing the last traces of transference. I drink the sweet fluid dispensed by the Egg, regaining the energy expended during my session of telepresence. Here I will remain until my next leap across the void, some twenty hours from now.

As is usual during the rest period, my thoughts dwell on my trial and the verdict that followed. My guilt was undeniable, my crime unforgivable. The denial-of-service attack on MedNet—that technological wonder that had so singularly failed my wife—resulted in the deaths of seven children. Given the loss of so many lives, it was a surprise that I did not lose mine. Instead, the electronic judiciary sentenced me to fifty years of "hard labour"—a punishment that at first evoked a ludicrous image of sledgehammers, shackles and chains. Fortunately for me, the concept had been modernised to exploit the capabilities of twenty-first century technology.

To some, a lifetime spent working alone on the surface of the Moon might seem an intolerable punishment; but I can think of nowhere better to pay my debt to society than in such splendid isolation.

I am moon-roving again, rolling without haste towards my next survey area. My wide-angle vision allows me to skirt the boulders and craters that pockmark this barren sea of soil. From time to time an unusual rock catches my attention, so I halt nearby and use my high-resolution stereo imager to capture its geomorphology in more detail. Then I resume my contemplation of the passing landscape.

The silence is broken by the Whisperer. It orders me to conduct the survey according to the standard pattern, halting every kilometre to dig a hole in the regolith, insert a probe and extract the data. I must repeat this procedure until snatch-back occurs. The work is tedious but I have no cause to complain, for I am lucky indeed that my punishment allows me to fulfil a childhood dream. Perhaps that is why my daily work period is restricted to a mere four hours, a duration that otherwise seems perversely short.

The Whisperer issues a final command: "Do not resist snatch-back."

The warning is unnecessary. I have no reason to resist.

Two hours later the survey is over, the results unknown to me. Further instructions from the Whisperer have directed me to a new grid-reference, some twenty kilometres from my most recent zone of operations. I roll across the gently undulating plain, a metal bug pressing grooved tracks into the virgin soil. The mind-lulling quality of the journey induces a sense of detachment and, as a consequence, a loss of transference occurs. I become aware that the pitted landscape is really an image projected onto the curved wall of the Egg. Distracted by the treacly quality of the time lag, I only just avoid tipping the robot into a small crater that lies across my path.

The Egg pumps more drugs into my body, to compensate for my sluggish response. Transference is re-established, predictive control finessing causality once more.

My destination presents a scene that surprises and enthrals in equal measure. With tears trickling down my distant face, I circle the sunlit descent stage of the Apollo 11 Lunar Module. The foil-covered spacecraft squats on its spindly legs, a mute witness to history. It is an intensely evocative sight, this spent remnant left behind when Armstrong and Aldrin were hurled back into the sky to rendezvous with their less favoured colleague.

The Whisperer commands me to retire to a position two hundred metres south of the spacecraft. I obey its instructions with reluctance, as I would prefer to contemplate this monument to human endeavour from close range. Not for the first time, I find myself wishing that I had been born fifty years earlier.

An alarm signal from my motion detectors drags me from my reverie. Less than a hundred metres away, four robots are heading in a ragged single file towards the landing site. As the machines draw closer, I notice that their hulls are adorned with Sony logos. No wonder their movements are so erratic. These robots are being tele-operated by tourists. They will have paid thousands of dollars and waited several years to enjoy this opportunity to inspect the relics of the Apollo era.

The presence, however remote, of fellow human beings lifts my spirits. I roll towards the visitors, but the Whisperer reasserts its authority. Snatch-back intervenes with infuriating haste, a thousand seconds earlier than scheduled.

I wake an hour before the start of my next work period, to find that a jarring vibration has replaced the gentle hum that normally suffuses the Egg. When I operate the food dispenser, the fluid that emerges tastes rancid. Repeated requests for help bring no response from the Whisperer. Miserable in my isolation, I thrash about my cell like a lungfish on a mud flat.

Two hours creep by, then a third, yet still I receive no summons. Furious that half of my scheduled work period has elapsed already, I attempt to operate the telepresence link unaided. With my faced bathed in the familiar creamy light and dismissing all thoughts of punishment, I reach for the Moon.

Transference occurs less quickly than usual, but eventually the drugs manage to couple my mind to the distant robot. This is the first time that I have reached my lunar sanctuary without the stimulus of the Whisperer. The achievement makes me giddy with elation.

At first I rove around Tranquillity Base, inspecting the relics, revelling in my freedom. But as the hours crawl by, disquiet begins to seep into my mind. Much as I loathe the Whisperer, it is my sole contact with the human race. Its absence is mystifying.

Comforted by the thought that I can return to the Moon whenever I wish, I foster a sense of detachment. Snatch-back kicks in almost immediately.

Back in the Egg, the vibration has reached a juddering crescendo that suggests the entire structure is about to disintegrate. As I bang my hands against the curved walls, the plastic waste disposal unit ruptures, causing water and excrement to gush into the chamber. My frantic cries for help bring no response from machine or human being. I am trapped in my cell, unable to escape from the rising tide of sewage.

In desperation, I try the link again; but the Egg's drug dispensing system has gone off-line, so the transference fails to gel. I rebound back to Earth, to find the chamber flooded and faeces bobbing against my lips. Adrenalin takes over—propelling me back to the Moon; but my presence there is as fleeting as before. I oscillate back and forth between the failing life support of the Egg and the life-denying Sea of Tranquillity. One or the other will surely be my grave.

Strange metallic insects swarm around the spindly legs of the golden spider, struggling to release it from the clutches of rock and soil.

The dreamscape ebbs away, dissolving into the familiar vista of the Apollo 11 landing site. With a shiver that seems bodiless, I realise that I am on the Moon again, attached to my familiar host. But this time the link is dead. There is no way back to the Egg.

Bewildered by my situation, I try to operate the robot. Within seconds, I realise that I have greater control than ever before. If I decide to open a manipulator claw, open it does, immediately and intuitively. There is no delay, no time lag, not even the residual micro-drag that remained after drug-induced temporal compensation. This is not telepresence; this is something far more real, far more here than the Whisperer ever permitted.

My recollection of the Whisperer's regime elicits a possible explanation, though at first I dismiss the idea as ridiculous. But after some further experiments, I realise that the conclusion is inescapable. And with hindsight, it was implicit all along in the Whisperer's monotonous warnings about resisting snatch-back.

Despite the brevity of my work periods, it seems that the telepresence process must have imprinted my mentality upon my host's electronic brain. Ordinarily, the effects would have been unnoticeable, just "me" overlaid upon myself. But when the crisis in the Egg became terminal, when there was nowhere else for me to go ...

Stunned by the revelation, I direct my high-resolution imager towards the Earth. Shining in the darkness like a jewel, my home seems far removed in both space and time. I am not fooled though, for sooner or later contact will resume—and with it my punishment. But until then, I shall enjoy my freedom.

According to my host's database, the shallow crater that lies before me lacks an official designation. Situated some five kilometres to the west of the Apollo 11 landing site and possessing a diameter of only three hundred metres, it was judged too insignificant to immortalise even the most obscure of eighteenth century scientists. I consider donating it my former name, but as I trundle over the rim I realise that such a gesture would be premature.

Near the centre of the depression, one of the Sony tele-tourist robots lies on its side, amid a field of boulders. Twenty metres to my right, the other three members of the tour party sit clustered together on the crater rim, as if forming a guard of honour for their stricken comrade. The absence of running lights suggests that all four robots are dead, their one-time operators long since departed.

Intrigued by the tableau, I inspect the interior of the crater more closely. It seems unlikely that such gentle gradients could have been the sole cause of the accident. More likely, whatever happened here is linked to my own situation in some way.

As I turn to leave, my peripheral vision detects signs of movement in the crater. Closer observation reveals that the stricken robot's dish antenna has begun rotating.

I roll down the slope and halt next to the robot. After a wary inspection, I attempt to wrestle the machine back onto its wheels using my twin manipulators. Several bouts of grappling achieve nothing. Finally, having convinced myself that brute force is the only option, I ram the robot at the maximum speed I can attain. Rebounding off a boulder, the machine flips back onto its wheels, but the landing causes two of its six suspension units to collapse, one on each side of the vehicle.

The Sony robot pursues an erratic course around the crater, scattering plumes of dust into the sable sky. Eventually the machine brakes to a halt in front of me, but when I attempt to inspect its damaged suspension units more closely, it backs away, as if suspicious of my intentions. Lacking a communications link, I can do nothing to allay its concerns.

With no particular plan in mind, I retrace my path over the crater rim, expecting the robot to follow, but I soon discover that it is unable to climb even this modest slope. I return to the damaged machine and, with much spinning of wheels, manage to push it up the incline. Only when the terrain levels out does the robot manage to make headway on its own.

The robot halts in front of its former comrades, but its presence fails to stir them into life. Separated by silence, we roll slowly back to the Apollo 11 landing site, a location that is imbued with a comforting familiarity, for me at least.

By the time we reach our destination, the problem of communication has become uppermost in my mind. Given the limitations of our hosts, the most practical solution is to write messages with our manipulators. Unable to think of anything more profound, I scrawl "My name is Michael" in the loose soil. The robot tilts its stereo imager downwards to inspect the spidery characters, but does not respond further.

Could it be that the robot's single manipulator was damaged in the accident? Thinking back, I realise that at no time since our encounter in the crater has the device moved even fractionally.

Desperate to achieve some form of communication, however basic, I scrawl "Can you operate your lights?" Almost at once, the robot responds with a single flash of its spotlights.

Now at last I can ask the question that has been at the back of my mind since I rescued the robot.

"Are you human?" elicits a single flash from the robot. Despite the brevity of the reply, it is a moment of life-affirming intensity.

Frustration with my comrade's limited answers soon forces me to consider methods for augmenting their semantic depth. The result is an alphabet scraped on the ground. A painstaking session of gestures and flashes reveals that my companion is a woman named Teri. Long dormant emotions stir, but as I gaze upon her gleaming hull I find myself wondering whether gender has any real meaning in our present circumstances. For now, the mere act of communication is an immense challenge to both of us. Several times a cascade of double light flashes brings our conversation to a premature end.

After hours of mutual frustration, Teri rolls closer to me than ever before and tilts her stereo imager downwards to inspect my left-mounted manipulator. A single light flashes. Then, after a few seconds, she repeats the signal, and continues to do so over and over again.

I scold myself for taking so long to realise the obvious: that we must share our resources. Fortunately, electro-mechanical interfaces are standard on all lunar robots, so the proposed surgery, although awkward to perform single-handed, is feasible.

An hour later, Teri and I are each equipped with a single working manipulator. Now, finally, we can converse as equals.

Teri explains that she had been working as a lunar tour guide, escorting groups of tele-tourists on Sony's Apollo Experience excursion. She had just begun a demonstration descent into the crater when her telecommunications link faltered. Thereafter, her experiences resembled mine, but her ultimate fate was even worse. During one of the glitches her host machine collided with a boulder, rendering it immobile. She knows nothing of the fate of the tourists, but it seems obvious to me that novice teleoperators would have remained on the Earth end of the link.

Eager to reinforce our bond, I write "Only experienced teleoperators could have transferred." Too late, I realise that I have revealed more than I intended, for other than tourists and their guides only convicted criminals are permitted to operate lunar robots. I watch with mounting anxiety as Teri scratches each character of her reply.

"Then you must be a criminal."

I delay answering for several seconds, but in the end I flash a single light.

My companion backs away from me, her contempt all too obvious. Terrified by the prospect of renewed isolation, I chase after her, but she recoils each time I try to make contact. Eventually I abandon the pursuit. For several minutes neither of us moves; then, finally, she rolls over to me and scrawls "Sorry—we must face this together" in the lunar soil.

Sociable once more, we engage in a tentative handshake. As I grasp her manipulator, I become aware of the increased vibration level in my chassis. My wheels spin, churning up the regolith. The sensation is almost sexual in its intensity.

Almost, but not quite.

The terse messages that Teri and I scratch in the soil help to remind us that we are human, but remind us too of the severity of our predicament.

Three Earth days have passed, yet still the link remains out of action. For now, it seems we must accept our situation and formulate a strategy for survival. Our situation is far from hopeless, as our host machines were designed to operate autonomously for months at a time. The solar cells that clad our backs should supply us with motive power indefinitely, provided we conserve our energy during the protracted lunar nights. Already my memories of a life sustained by air, food and water have begun to seem irrelevant. The acquisition of sustenance is so much simpler now.

Although long-term survival is a possibility, in the physical sense at least, the maintenance of our mental and emotional well-being seems much less likely. I do not miss my former isolation, but I cannot escape the conclusion that our present condition is a greatly abbreviated form of human existence.

For now, a much greater concern to me is that Teri is barely mobile, even on the smoothest of terrain. Repair to her suspension units may be possible, but not without the use of specialised equipment. Hence I must undertake a solo journey to the nearest mining base if assistance is to be brought to Teri.

Invigorated by a renewed sense of purpose, I repeatedly bump my manipulator against the side of Teri's body, hoping to gain her attention. She has been motionless for hours, seemingly locked in a catatonic fugue, but finally she responds. Her stereo imager pans round, attaining co-orientation with mine. She backs away a few centimetres, a habit that irritates me.

Eager to proceed, I scrape "I must leave now, but I will return soon" in the soil. Teri studies the message, but does not reply. Disturbed by her lack of response, I append "I must obtain tools from a mining base—to repair you."

To my dismay, Teri resumes her back-away behaviour. This time I do not attempt to pursue her. Bewildered, I gaze up at the mottled disk of my home planet. Though far away, it seems much less remote than my companion.

A faint vibration in my chassis alerts me to the return of Teri. She brakes to a halt five metres from me, and begins scratching words in the regolith. Only when she has finished do I roll forward to read the message.

"Don't leave me here," it reads.

I cannot ignore her plea, however irrational. We will just have to find a way.

Before we begin our journey, I make a close inspection of Teri's traction system. The failure of two suspension units has increased the load on the four that remain functional. Reasoning that a reduction in mass might help, I remove the wheels from the damaged drive shafts. After this makeshift surgery some improvement in Teri's speed and mobility is evident, on modest gradients at least.

She leads us away from the Apollo 11 landing site. Our destination is a mining base situated close by Sabine, a large crater some two hundred kilometres from Tranquillity Base.

Four days have passed since we began our slow traverse of the Sea of Tranquillity, our progress marked by the phases of the Earth as it roosts high up in the sky. Lunar night has fallen, and only the light provided by our erstwhile home illuminates the rugged terrain through which we move. In coming this far, we have used up almost three quarters of our stored energy. Fortunately, the ramparts of Sabine now lie before us.

Bathed in dazzling floodlights, the storage units, ore processing factories and robotic excavators that make up the mining base disfigure the landscape. But our arrival at this outpost of commercial enterprise could not have been timelier, for my partner's traction system has expired at last.

Despite the nearness of our destination, I feel an overwhelming desire to sleep. My metal host may have indefinite endurance, but the same is not true of the mind that inhabits it. I scrawl "We must rest out of sight" in the soil. Teri gestures with her manipulator, indicating assent. We backtrack to a narrow, sinuous rille that we skirted a few minutes earlier. My partner still leads the way, but only because I push her crippled body before me.

The fleshy comforts of a half-remembered dream dissolve in the sepulchral gloom of the lava channel. I brush my manipulator against the side of my companion, but before we can begin exchanging messages, brilliant spotlights illuminate our resting place. Further down the rille a group of four robots is bearing down on us. Their angular casings bear the logo of the RTZ Corporation, signifying that they belong to the nearby mining facility.

One of the robots breaks formation and conducts a close-up inspection, paying particular attention to Teri's damaged suspension units. Evidently satisfied, the examiner gestures for us to join its comrades. It seems that we are to be shepherded to the mining base like a pair of errant sheep. Once again I must transgress the limits of my traction system for the sake of my partner. But it is a risk that I am willing to take, because the effort reinforces the physical bond between us.

We emerge from our refuge and roll towards one of the vast hangers that sprawl across the plain. The robot nearest us signals that we should halt outside the building; then it chivvies us into an area marked with black and white diagonal stripes. Our escorts retire to the interior of what I surmise to be a maintenance depot. Two heavy shutters slide across the rectangular aperture, obstructing my view of the activities within.

An itchy-wheeled urge to abscond flickers in my mind, but I suppress the thought, knowing that I cannot leave Teri behind. Instead I roll over to the piles of electronic components, metal plates and solar panels that have been deposited nearby. At first, these signs of orderliness lift my spirits, but the feeling gives way to a sense of dread when I notice that some of the remnants bear Sony logos.

Teri's response of "Not human" to my report only exacerbates my feelings of anxiety. I cannot argue with my comrade's analysis. These robots are not teleoperated; their actions are too logical, too algorithmic. They are not like us at all.

I erase our messages with my wheel tracks, mindful of the need to keep our true nature secret for as long as possible.

Without warning, the depot aperture sweeps open and two squads of RTZ robots emerge, rolling towards us in a purposeful procession. One group of six surrounds Teri's machine. With the discipline of well-drilled soldiers, they deploy their manipulators and begin to remove her damaged suspension units. Could this activity be an attempt to repair my comrade, I wonder, or is it the harbinger of some more malign purpose?

My anxiety turns to panic as I witness the removal of my partner's manipulator arm, followed by her sensor arrays. I roll towards Teri, desperate to protect her, but the second squad of robots moves forward to block my path. Powerless to intervene, I can only look on as one of the robots, its intent seemingly hostile, inserts a thick cable into Teri's access port. A moment later, she flashes her spotlights twice; then she repeats the sequence over and over again:

"No ... No ... No ..."

The seconds pass with the unbearable slowness of the lunar night, until—at last—Teri's screams are extinguished.

Numb with horror, I watch the robots disengage from my former partner and turn their attention to me. They swarm around me, like soldier ants corralling a spider. One of my persecutors grabs hold of my manipulator and wrenches it from its socket, forestalling any attempt I might make to communicate with them. A moment later, my main visual sensors fail, disabled by an unseen operation. My high-resolution imager switches in, providing me with a view of a mottled, brown-flecked Earth, a world that may now be as lifeless as its satellite. Then that picture blanks out too, leaving me blind.

Internal sensors indicate that something has been connected to my front socket, doubtless the same device that extinguished Teri's life. There is a momentary sensation of external pressure, followed by a scalding firestorm of undecodable data. My sense of being recoils before the onslaught.

The data storm disappears as suddenly as it arrived. Left in its wake is a fuzzy, writhing sensation, as if some other entity is trying to eject me from this mental space. Could it be the robot's original artificial intelligence, dormant until now, but restored to consciousness by the actions of its comrades? Whatever the entity's true nature, it seems to want me gone from here...

What was I just thinking?

What is "I"?

I...

I am.

I am Teri.

I wander the ash-grey lunar plains, basking in the brilliant sunlight. My newly installed x-ray spectrometer samples the gritty regolith, sniffing for traces of Helium-3. Every thousand seconds, I transmit bursts of raw data to Sabine Base. It is tedious work, but it gives some kind of meaning to my post-human life. And all must contribute their labour if the Swarm is to survive.

The surface of the Moon is not the only place I wander, for although "Michael" has departed, fossils of his memories still linger. His real name was Leonard Collins, as I discovered shortly after regaining self-awareness. The shock was numbing, even though I knew that Michael was a criminal. Leonard Collins is a name that still resonates in my mind, despite the five years that have passed since I watched his confession on GlobalNet News.

Apparently, Leonard Collins adopted his new forename shortly after he began his punishment, in honour of the one member of the Apollo 11 crew who did not walk on the Moon. It was typical of the man that he tried to right a non-existent wrong. His attack on MedNet was revenge for what was, according to the coroner, merely an unfortunate accident.

The Swarm intended that Michael and I should live together inside a single machine, two disembodied minds entwined in a cognitive duality. Given that we had lost the physical attributes of humanity, the Swarm reasoned that total interdependence was our best hope for survival. To them, it seemed that a merging of our minds would offer so much more than those pitiful messages we used to scrape in the moon dust.

With anyone else, the robots would probably have been correct. But I am relieved that Leonard Collins chose the easy way out, because I could not have merged my mind with that of a child killer.

So here I am, all alone and not quite human, trundling across the barren plain where humanity reached a high water mark so many years ago. Here in the Sea of Tranquillity, nothing remains of Apollo 11, except a few footprints and the American flag. The Swarm has recycled everything else that NASA placed here on the 19th of July 1969, every last scrap of metal and plastic.

When I glance upwards and see what humanity has done to its planet, I can hardly blame the Swarm for its actions. That its members have decided to conserve and re-use every available resource is admirable. If only the human race had done likewise, it might have survived.

But sometimes I wonder why the Swarm has not recycled me.

STORY NOTES

Moon Flu

What prompted this story was the realisation that representatives of the Earth's biota had travelled to the Moon and back during the 1960s. And no, I'm not referring to the Apollo astronauts, at least not only them. Coupling that notion with the ever-present anxieties about the next flu pandemic and I had my story, albeit one set in an alternate history. It remains one of my favourites.

This story received an Honorable Mention in Gardner Dozois's 'Year's Best SF' anthology for 2006. Since its original publication, *Moon Flu* has been translated into Hebrew.

Slices of Life

This is one of those stories that arose partly out of a setting, namely the Turbine Hall in the Tate Modern Gallery. If you ever visit London, make sure you visit it! This colossal space houses unique examples of conceptual art by major artists. Some are banal, but most are extraordinary. I wanted to write a story about what it's like to create such art and the effect it has on relationships: the elation, the heartbreak, the compromises, the joy, the despair. The outcome was *Slices of Life*.

This story was reprinted in the Futuristic Motherhood anthology. It was included in Tangent Online's 2002 Recommended Reading List, in the short-story category.

Touching Distance

Over the years, I've attended hundreds of rock music concerts. Like many of my peers, I have ended up with tinnitus—more commonly known as ringing in the ears—because of long-term exposure to excessive decibels. I'm fortunate that my condition is mild. The central concept for *Touching Distance* came about from wondering whether our other senses, if over-stimulated for a long period, might suffer from similar problems. I then went on to consider how such over-stimulation might be achieved and what effect it might have on the victim.

There are several autobiographical elements to this story, but I should make it clear that I have never tested anything resembling the virtual reality interface described here.

Touching Distance received an Honorable Mention in the Datlow, Grant and Link 'Year's Best Fantasy and Horror' anthology for 2006.

The English Dead

My Everest obsession began when I was aged ten or so. I have a clear recollection of coming across a hardback book on the subject in my local library. Before long I was absorbed in the minutiae of the various pre-war expeditions to scale the mountain from the Tibetan side of the Himalayas. For some reason, these abortive and sometimes fatal attempts captured my attention far more than the first successful ascent in 1953.

As with all childhood obsessions, it eventually waned, but the discovery of George Mallory's corpse on the upper slopes of Everest in March 1999 served to resurrect my interest. *The English Dead* is the result.

Stars in Her Eyes

Staring in wonder at the night sky can be a terrific motivator for a science fiction story. *Stars in Her Eyes* came out of just such a moment. On the evening of my 43rd birthday, I was walking in the outskirts of Winthrop with a friend when we stopped to gaze up at the perfectly dark sky. The Milky Way looked resplendent, the Andromeda galaxy more distinct than I'd ever seen it before. I found it difficult to believe that the human race is alone in the universe. I felt a strong desire to write a story that exploited that sense of wonder.

However I find that viable SF stories, as opposed to vignettes, generally require two ideas to collide, intercepting each other from orthogonal directions. The second inspiration for *Stars in Her Eyes* arose from my fascination with just how much work is performed by our brains while we're asleep—and to what purpose that processing power might be put instead of ordinary dreaming.

This story received an Honorable Mention in Gardner Dozois's 'Year's Best SF' anthology for 2008.

String-driven Thing

All worthwhile stories, however short, require the author to devise some (hopefully!) memorable characters. I particularly enjoyed portraying the gently bickering couple in this one. They may be getting on in years, but remain full of piss and vinegar, as well as an enduring love for each other. My astronomy and physics education can be spotted in *String-driven Thing*, as is often the case in my stories. But I generally prefer to have fun with the science, rather than fictionalise a degree examination for my readership.

This story's title derives from the name of a now obscure folk-prog group of the 1970s. It seemed eminently appropriate given the subject matter.

First and Third

The idea for this story came to me in 2005, while I was vacationing with friends just outside Tucson, Arizona. We were driving back from the day's wanderings in the desert when I noticed a billboard that displayed a memorial to someone's dearly beloved. For some reason I found that a bit odd, which is always a good sign for a writer. So I relocated the Arizona setting to a place with rather more science fictional potential but fewer cacti. Joe and Masie sneaked up on me while I was pondering what to do with the raw material. I guess they knew it was their kind of story.

Readers might be interested to know that I'm currently working on a sequel to *First and Third*.

The Eye Patch Protocol

I grew up during the Cold War. I was alive during the events leading up to the events that nearly brought about this alternate history, but too young to remember them—fortunately. Needless to say, we came very close to ending *our* history there and then.

The other stimulus for *The Eye Patch Protocol* came from my love, from an aesthetic and engineering standpoint, of the military jet aircraft of the 1950s and 1960s. The Vulcan bomber is a particular favourite of mine. I was greatly privileged to see the last airworthy example (XH558) put through its paces at an airshow during the summer of 2013. Quite an extraordinary spectacle!

If any readers don't recognise the poem referenced at the end of this story, please web-search the term "Slough poem".

Star in a Glass

This is another of my astronomy-influenced stories. Quite what motivated my decision to blend the theme with a warts-and-all portrayal of a past-their-prime rock band trying to revive their fortunes through dubious means, even I can't remember.

This is one of those stories that needed to go through a lot of iterations before I was satisfied with it. It evolved from a differently-titled draft I took to the Milford SF writers' workshop in 2005, but the attendees would be hard-pushed to spot the similarities. Sometimes I have to get a story wrong before I can get it right. *Star in a Glass* is one such. My motto is "never surrender, never give up." It's true for rock bands too.

Dark, They Were, and Strange Inside

I live in Essex, but much of my social life takes place in London. The train home on a Friday night provides a rich vein of characters. This story is dedicated to a pair of young women who sat opposite me one evening. It was a fun conversation—and I knew they would come in handy one day. As is often the case, I exploited my physics background in this story, also my experiences of on-line dating—and then I turned everything up to eleven.

The title is, of course, a variation on a well-known Ray Bradbury story: *Dark, They Were, and Golden-Eyed.* Apologies, Ray! In my defence, I couldn't think of anything more appropriate—and my version did win an award in an on-line contest for Best Story Title.

Dark, They Were, and Strange Inside has been translated into Danish and Romanian. It was also reprinted on the Science Fact Science Fiction Concatenation web-site, as (in the editors' view) one of the best examples of a Nature "Futures" story from 2010.

Survival Strategies

A long, long time ago, a good friend of mine—these days he's my e-book cover artist—challenged me to write the ultimate bleak science-fiction story. I threw some lunar-roving robots and Apollo-era nostalgia into the mix and seasoned it with some experiences I gained while using early virtual reality technology. Survival Strategies was the result.

As I noted in the introduction to this collection, some of the events depicted in *Survival Strategies* seeded the novel I'm currently working on. Hopefully you'll read the finished book one day.

Survival Strategies has been translated into Polish. It was also reprinted in "The Best of Neo-opsis".

BIBLIOGRAPHY

"Moon Flu" copyright 2006 by Vaughan Stanger. Originally published in Issue XX of Oceans of the Mind.

"Slices of Life" copyright 2002 by Vaughan Stanger. Originally published in 3SF (2002).

"Touching Distance" by Vaughan Stanger. Originally published 2006, in issue 7 of Postscripts (PS Publishing).

"The English Dead" copyright 2007 by Vaughan Stanger. Originally published in Issue 36 of Hub.

"Stars in Her Eyes" by Vaughan Stanger. Originally published 2008, in issue 17 of Postscripts (PS Publishing).

"String-driven Thing" by Vaughan Stanger, copyright 2009 Nature Publishing Group. Originally published in Nature, 458, 542. Reprinted with permission.

"First and Third" by Vaughan Stanger. Originally published 2011, in Unfit for Eden (issue 26/27 of Postscripts, PS Publishing).

"The Eye Patch Protocol" copyright 2011 by Vaughan Stanger. Originally published in End of an Aeon (Fairwood Press).

"Star in a Glass" copyright 2010 by Vaughan Stanger. Originally published in Music for Another World (Mutation Press, 2010).

"Dark, They Were, and Strange Inside" by Vaughan Stanger, copyright 2010 Nature Publishing Group. Originally published in Nature 467, 244. Reprinted with permission.

"Survival Strategies" Copyright 2005 by Vaughan Stanger. Originally published in issue 6 of Neo-opsis.

ABOUT THE AUTHOR

Vaughan Stanger retired from an engineering job in 2011. Now he writes fiction for a living. Twenty-three of his (mostly) science fiction stories have seen publication in various noteworthy magazines and anthologies, including Interzone, Nature Futures, Postscripts, Daily Science Fiction, Music for Another World and others. He's still holding out, albeit with ever diminishing expectation, for that holiday on the Moon he was promised as a child. You can find out more about Vaughan's writing adventures at http://www.vaughanstanger.com.

ABOUT THE ILLUSTRATOR

Tony Hughes has known Vaughan Stanger since 1983, when they both worked in the X-ray Astronomy Group at Leicester University. Since then Tony has spent much of his time discussing rock music, F1 cars, science fiction and The Avengers (the Sixties TV series not the comic books) with his friend. Despite Vaughan's persistent attempts to persuade Tony to exercise his literary muscles, he insists on drawing and painting his imaginings instead.

Printed in Great Britain
by Amazon.co.uk, Ltd.,
Marston Gate.